BIRD TRACKS IN THE AIR

Selected Poems of Wang Anshi

空鸟迹

王安石诗词中英本

[加] 王健（Jan W. Walls）
李盈（Yvonne L. Walls） 编译 柳玲玲 绘图

新世界出版社
NEW WORLD PRESS

First Edition 2019

Compiled and translated by Jan W. Walls & Yvonne L. Walls
Illustrated by Liu Lingling
Book Design by He Yuting

ISBN 978-7-5104-6810-0

Published by
NEW WORLD PRESS
24 Baiwanzhuang Street, Beijing 100037, China

Distributed by
NEW WORLD PRESS
24 Baiwanzhuang Street, Beijing 100037, China
Tel: 86-10-68995968
Fax: 86-10-68998705
Website: www.nwp.com.cn
E-mail: nwpcd@sina.com

Printed in the People's Republic of China

PREFACE

Why would we want to publish English translations of 130 poems and lyrics by an 11th century man who is best known as a statesman, a political, economic, military and educational reformer? As a writer, Wang Anshi (1021-1086) has always been known as an essayist, one of the "Eight Great Essayists of the Tang and Song Dynasties," but it turns out that, especially in his later years, he was a master of the shorter verse forms, the eight-line regulated verse (lǜshī) and the quatrain verse (juéjù) forms. We believe that the quality of these poems earns him the right to be called one of the truly great poets of the Song dynasty.

To better understand Wang's sense of determination and commitment to follow through his projects in spite of resistance from his peers, we only need to review one of his more famous essays, the "Record of an Excursion to Mount Baochan," written in 1054 when Wang was 33 years old, still a young official. One day, he and four relatives and friends visited a cave about three kilometers beyond the famous Huayan Cave in Mount Baochan (also known as Mount Hua, located in today's Anhui Province), Wang wrote the following:

前言

王安石（1021—1086）是中国11世纪著名的思想家、政治家、改革家。我们为什么要翻译他的130首诗词呢？因为他也是有名的文学家。就文学而言，王安石以散文家著称，是“唐宋八大家”之一。此外，他还是律诗和绝句的大家，晚年的诗词更是他的代表性作品。因之，我们觉得他可以被称为宋代伟大的诗人之一，应该把他的作品翻译成英文，以供英文读者欣赏。

为了了解王安石的诗词，我们首先需要了解为什么在同仁都极力反对的情况下，他还要坚决实施变法政策。只要看一下1054年他写的《游褒禅山记》就会更清楚了，那时33岁的他还是一个小官。一天，他与四位亲朋好友在褒禅山（今安徽省境内，旧名花山）游玩，走到离华严洞三里外无人知晓的岩洞。他写道：

I went in with four others, carrying torches. The deeper we went, the harder it was to advance and the more marvelous the sights became. One person who had grown sluggish and wanted to go back, said "If we don't go back now our torches will die out!" So we had no choice but to withdraw with him. We probably had explored less than one-tenth of the distance that more daring explorers had reached, but even so, when we looked around the cave walls, we noticed that records left by earlier visitors had already become fewer. Most likely even fewer people had plumbed the greater depths. At that point I still had the strength to go farther in, and the torches could still last long enough, so after we came out there was some blaming of the one who had wanted to turn back. I also regretted following him before enjoying the sense of fulfillment in exploring as far as we could.

I sighed with regret over this! Ancient people learned so much from observing heaven and earth, mountains and streams, grass and trees, insects, fish, birds and beasts, because they explored deeply and widely. Flatlands that are nearby attract plenty of travelers, but few ever visit places that are distant and challenging. But the world's most marvelous, magnificent, rare and unusual sights are most often found in those dangerous, out-of-the-way places that people seldom reach. People who lack willpower cannot reach such places; nor can those who have the willpower to not stop just because others have stopped, but lack the stamina to go on; nor can those who have both willpower and stamina, and do not become sluggish just because others do, but have nothing to guide them once they reach the remote and puzzling depths.

余与四人拥火以入，入之愈深，其进愈难，而其见愈奇。有怠而欲出者，曰：“不出，火且尽。”遂与之俱出。盖余所至，比好游者尚不能十一，然视其左右，来而记之者已少。盖其又深，则其至又加少矣。方是时，余之力尚足以入，火尚足以明也。既其出，则或咎其欲出者，而余亦悔其随之而不得极夫游之乐也。

于是余有叹焉。古人之观于天地、山川、草木、虫鱼、鸟兽，往往有得，以其求思之深而无不在也。夫夷以近，则游者众；险以远，则至者少。而世之奇伟、瑰怪、非常之观，常在于险远，而人之所罕至焉，故非有志者不能至也。有志矣，不随以止也，然力不足者，亦不能至也。有志与力，而又不随以怠，至于幽暗昏惑而无物以相之，亦不能至也。

——摘自：《临川先生文集·游褒禅山记》

It shows that Wang had the willpower, the stamina, and the vision for a better China in the implementation of his New Policies reform, in spite of the vehement and on-going opposition from his conservative colleagues.

After passing the Imperial Examination in 1042, Wang Anshi spent the next 16 years serving in regional posts in the Jiangnan regions (today's Jiangxi and Anhui provinces). Even in his earlier years in regional office, Wang always had the whole country in mind. This time in the southern region gave him ample opportunity to observe the iniquity and suffering imposed on the peasantry by ruthless landlords and corrupt local officials. His sympathy for those who suffered, and his antipathy toward those who cause the suffering, are abundantly revealed in many of his poems composed in the years prior to his retirement. They include such poems as "Moved by Events" (#31), "Countryside Stroll" (#33), "Land Grabbing" (#34) and "Confiscating Salt" (#35). His heartfelt sympathy for the common folk, and his belief that their condition could be improved through better government, all expressed through his poems, are the concerns of a very serious Confucianist.

由此可见，王安石知道，要施行新法，一定要有意志、毅力和远见。尽管保守派不断反对新法，为了建造更美好的国家，王安石仍坚决实施变法政策。

1042 年，通过科举考试以后，有 16 年的时间，他只在江南（今江西、安徽）做地方官。在做地方官的时候，他已经想到治理全国了。这一时期，他有很多机会可以亲眼观察到残酷的地主和腐败的地方官僚对农民不平等的待遇使他们受难、吃苦。对受难者的同情和对压迫者的反感表现在他隐退前的许多诗词中，如《感事》（31*）、《郊行》（33）、《兼并》（34）和《收盐》（35）。他的诗词所表露的意念认为，一个好的政府可以改进到像他那样能同情一般的苦难民众。这正是非常儒家的思想。

---

* 括号中的数字为该诗在本书中的编号。

It was after his retirement from office, and witnessing the wholesale dismantling of his comprehensive political, economic, educational, social and military reforms, that the Taoistic and Buddhistic dimensions of his worldview were revealed through his poetry. Most critics have agreed that his best poems are those eight-line regulated verses (lǜshī) and four-line quatrains (juéjù) composed during the post-retirement phase of his life. Wang's love and respect for Nature, for natural phenomena, for the beauty, grandeur and power of Nature as opposed to the machinations of the dusty world of society, all reveal the mindset of an indisputable Taoist. Poems like "Plum Tree about to Bloom by the Waterway" (#69), "Tree Tips" (#73), "North Mountain" (#74) and "A Sketch" (#77) reveal typical concerns of Wang's Taoist side.

Wang was, perhaps even more than a committed Taoist, a serious Chan (Zen) Buddhist. His quest for enlightenment, his sympathy for people and animals who suffer, his frequent visits to Buddhist temples, his appreciative poems to Buddhist monks and his many poems in imitation of the Buddhist monk-poets Han Shan and Shi De, all show him to be a serious believer in Buddhist ideals. This side of him is well illustrated by the following poems: "Twenty Poems in the Style of Han Shan and Shi De (Eleventh of 20 poems)" (#98), "Inscription on the Wall of Halfway Mountain Temple (Second of two poems)" (#102), "Ghost Town" (#107), "On the Occasion of Watching Actors" (#123), "Climbing Baogong Pagoda" (#126), and "To Master Li " (#129).

隐退以后，眼看着他的政治、经济、教育、社会和军事上的改革被全盘撤销，王安石的诗词更显现出道家和佛家的宇宙观。多数的文学批评家都认同这点——他隐退后的律诗和绝句是他最好的诗词。他对大自然、自然现象、大自然的伟大和大自然的力量的喜爱和佩服，对尘世社会的呆板的厌恶都表现出他的道家思想。例如：《沟上梅花欲发》（69）、《木末》（73）、《北山》（74）和《即事》（77）等。

王安石更是认真的禅佛家。他寻求觉悟、同情受苦的人和动物、经常造访佛寺、喜爱佛家的诗词并模仿诗僧寒山和拾得的诗等，均表现出他深信禅佛的意念。下列的诗词可以证实这一点：《拟寒山拾得二十首（其十一）》（98）、《题半山寺壁（二首之二）》（102）、《孤城》（107）、《相国寺启向天节道场行香院观戏者》（123）、《登宝公塔》（126）、《寄李道人》（129）。

In light of the above, we may say that Wang Anshi was a "Three Teachings Disciple": a Confucianist for social, political and economic affairs, a Taoist for his love of Nature, and a Buddhist in his commitment to achieving enlightenment for the relief of suffering. But for purposes of this book, he was an outstanding poet, recognized as such even by those who were totally opposed to his reform policies. He excelled in technical mastery of regulated verse and quatrains, but the flow of his words is so natural that the reciter or chanter is unaware that structural demands are being addressed, which allows us to focus on the poem's content and its meaning.

For all the above reasons, Wang's poetry deserves to be more widely appreciated, and we hope this book will contribute to that cause.

因之，我们可以说王安石是“三教徒”。因为，在社会、政治和经济事务方面，他是儒家；在喜爱大自然方面，他是道家；在追求解除痛苦、达到觉悟方面，他是佛家。然而，以我们的书而言，他是伟大的诗人。就连坚决反对他的变法政策的人也不得不承认这一点。在律诗和绝句的技巧方面他绝对是大师。他的字句非常流畅，使人不必注意其结构，而专注在内容和意思方面。

由于以上各种原因，王安石的诗词应该受到广泛的欣赏。我们仅此希望这本书能在这方面有所贡献。

CONTENTS

目录

The world was never made;
It will change, but it will not fade.
So let the wind range;
For even and morn
Ever will be
Thro' eternity.
Nothing was born;
Nothing will die;
All things will change.

– Alfred, Lord Tennyson (1809-1892),
from "Nothing Will Die"

导言

世界原就雄伟；
会变，但不凋萎。
让风伸展；
早与晚
将永远
替换。
万物非生；
万物永生；
万物恒变。

——〔英〕丁尼生 (1809—1892)，
选自《万物永生》

ABOUT WANG ANSHI

Wang Anshi (1021-1086), like his friend and political opponent Su Shi (Su Dongpo, 1037-1101), was "discovered" and recommended for promotion by Ouyang Xiu (1007-1072), the great writer and statesman of the Northern Song Dynasty. Historically, Wang Anshi himself was known as a prime minister. His controversial political, economic and military reform measures were vehemently opposed by so many government officials and powerful gentry that they would have been rescinded almost as soon as they were implemented were it not for the strong sympathy and support by the then emperor, Shen Zong.

As an essayist, Wang traditionally has been hailed as one of the "Eight Great Essayists of the Tang and Song Dynasties" together with Han Yu, Liu Zongyuan, Ouyang Xiu, Su Xun, Su Shi, Su Zhe and Zeng Gong, through whose personal recommendation Wang was "discovered" by Ouyang. As an arbiter of literary taste, Wang is usually credited with "discovering" Du Fu's true merit as "China's Greatest Poet." As a poet himself, Wang has been acknowledged to be, especially in his later years, one of the all-time great masters of the eight-line regulated verse (lǜshī) and the quatrain (juéjù) verse forms in particular. Thus, he certainly deserves to have representative poems made available in translation for an English language readership.

王安石：其人

王安石（1021—1086），如他的朋友和政治对手苏轼（苏东坡，1037—1101）一样，是被北宋的伟大文学家和政治家欧阳修（1007—1072）所“发掘”并推荐做官晋升的。在历史上，王安石本人以宰相闻名。他的许多政治、经济和军事方面的改革都受到政府官员和士绅的强烈反抗。要不是当时神宗的强力同情和支持，他一定无法实施这些政策。

作为散文家，王安石被称为“唐宋八大家”之一，与韩愈、柳宗元、欧阳修、苏洵、苏轼、苏辙和曾巩齐名。曾巩又是亲自把他介绍给欧阳修的人；由于曾巩的介绍，他才得以被“发掘”。作为诗歌的评论家，一般认为是他发现杜甫的真才并将其称为“中国最伟大的诗人”。以诗人而论，特别是晚年时，他被认为是律诗和绝句的大师。因之，他的代表性的诗词当然值得翻译成英文，以供世界读者学习与欣赏。

Wang's life and political career are too complex and important to be glossed over in a brief essay, but a chronology may be useful:

Age	Year	
	1021	Born in Linjiangjun (today's Qingjiang, Jiangxi Province). He was a native of Linchuan, Jiangxi;
9	1030	His father was appointed Prefect of Shaozhou (today's Shaoguan, Guangdong Province), Wang accompanied;
15	1036	His father returned to the capital (Bianjing, today's Kaifeng), Wang accompanied;
16	1037	His father was appointed Controller General of Jiangning (today's Nanjing), Wang accompanied;
18	1039	His father died; Wang entered mourning;
21	1042	Wang awarded Jin Shi (Advanced Scholar) Degree through the official examination system; was appointed to Yangzhou as Under-secretary to Military Commandant of Huainan for three year official apprenticeship;
25	1046	Having visited Linchuan after three years in Yangzhou, Wang returned to the Capital, refused an opportunity for major promotion, requested another regional office;
26	1047	Appointed as Magistrate to Yin County (today's Ningbo, Zhejiang Province); meritorious record;
30	1051	Appealed for delay of a commanded Special Examination; and was appointed as Controller General to Shuzhou (today's Anqing, Anhui Province);
32	1053	Ouyang Xiu strongly recommended Wang for promotion, which Wang declined;

王安石的生平和政治事业非常重要而复杂，其年表如下：

年龄	年代	
	1021	在临江军（今江西清江）出生。祖籍为江西临川。
9	1030	父王益以殿中丞知韶州（今广东韶关），王安石随父至韶州。
15	1036	父王益服满赴京（北宋京城汴京，今开封），王安石随行。
16	1037	父王益通判江宁府（今南京），王安石随行。
18	1039	父亲病逝；服丧。
21	1042	进士及第，至扬州，以秘书郎签书淮南节度判官厅公事三年。
25	1046	三年后赴临川，又自临川赴京。不求官职。宁为地方官。
26	1047	调鄞县（今浙江宁波）知县。成绩卓越。
30	1051	命参加考试，但要求延期。任舒州（今安徽安庆）通判。
32	1053	欧阳修极力上书推荐王安石晋升，但王拒绝。

33 1054 Again declined Ouyang Xiu's offer of opportunity for advancement, requesting another posting at provincial level; turned down another offer from Emperor for promotion to office in capital; turned down three other dispatches urging him to reconsider;

35 1056 Living in the capital, he accepted an appointment as a magistrate; appealed for another provincial posting;

36 1057 Was appointed as Prefect in Changzhou (in today's Jiangsu Province);

37 1058 Was appointed to as Chief Justice of Jiangdong Circuit (area covering portions of Anhui, Jiangsu and Zhejiang);

38 1059 Returned to capital to make annual work report; submitted "Myriad Word Memorial" to Emperor Ren Zong, calling for reform measures;

39 1060 Was appointed to Ministry of Works; lived in capital;

40 1061 Was appointed to the Ministry of Works as Director; refused to accept promotions;

41 1062 Several more refusals to accept promotion;

42 1063 Emperor Ren Zong died, succeeded on throne by Ying Zong; Wang's mother died; mourning period observed by Wang in Jiangning;

44 1065 During mourning period for mother, Wang was offered an appointment at the court of Emperor Ying Zong, but refused at least three times;

46 1067 Death of Ying Zong, accession of Emperor Shen Zong; Wang was appointed as Governor of Jiangning and Hanlin Academician;

47 1068 Was admitted to the capital by special decree; and gained the full confidence of Shen Zong;

33	1054	再次拒绝欧阳修推荐晋升，要求省级工作。拒绝皇帝提升京城之工作，并三次拒绝重新考虑的要求。
35	1056	接受群牧判官之职，身居京城，却要求省级工作。
36	1057	任常州（今江苏省）知府。
37	1058	任江东（包括安徽、江苏、浙江之部分）刑狱。
38	1059	返回京城述职。呈“万言书”给仁宗，提出变法主张。
39	1060	为工部郎中；居京城。
40	1061	任工部郎中；多次拒绝晋升。
41	1062	多次拒绝晋升；但仍为工部郎中，纠察在京刑狱，管干三班院。
42	1063	仁宗崩，英宗即位。王母逝世，居丧江宁。
44	1065	居丧期间，英宗朝廷屡次任命，但三次拒绝。
46	1067	英宗崩；神宗即位。诏王安石为江宁知府。再诏为翰林学士。
47	1068	受诏入京。深得神宗赏识。

48	1069	Was appointed as Vice Grand Counsellor; began introducing Reform Measures; opposition to reforms arose quickly; important officials began resigning office in protest;
49	1070	Was appointed as Prime Minister and Imperial Historiographer; more resignations by important officials protesting reforms;
51	1072	Wang started offering resignation in response to growing opposition and criticism; resignations repeatedly refused by Emperor Shen Zong;
53	1074	Wang resigned prime minister post, and was appointed as Governor of Jiangning; reform measures continued;
54	1075	Was recalled to be Prime Minister again, and Imperial Historiographe;
55	1076	Faced increasing personal and political problems in court; he resigned office in capital, and was appointed as Governor of Jiangning; he was gradually allowed to retire from office, and lived at Halfway Mountain (Ban Shan) midway between Jiangning (Nanjing) and Mount Zhong (Mount Bell);
56	1077	Was granted honorary title of "Duke of Shu";
59	1080	Was granted honorary title of "Duke of Jing";
64	1085	Death of Emperor Shen Zong; succession by Zhe Zong; Wang was offered honorary appointment as Minister of Works; Reform Measures rescinded one after another;
65	1086	Wang died in fourth month; title of Grand Tutor was bestowed posthumously. Known as "Wang, Duke Wen."

48	1069	出任参知政事。实施变法。随即受到反抗，多名重要官员辞职。
49	1070	任宰相；任史馆大学士，立保甲法，更多重要官员因反抗变法而辞职。
51	1072	王因更多反抗和批评要求罢相位，但屡屡遭神宗拒绝。
53	1074	罢宰相位。出知江宁府。变法继续。
54	1075	被召回任，二次拜相，同平章事，并拜左仆射，门下侍郎，复任诏章馆大学士。
55	1076	在朝廷进一步面临个人与政治困难。辞去京城之职；以使相镇金陵。子雱卒。渐允其退出职位。居江宁与钟山间之“半山”。
56	1077	封为舒国公。
59	1080	封荆国公。变法盛行。
64	1085	神宗崩；哲宗即位。加为司空；变法一一废除。
65	1086	四月病逝钟山；赠太傅，获谥“文”，世称王文公。

After having passed the Advanced Scholar (jìnshì) examinations, Wang served three years as a junior official. Noted for his repeated refusal to accept invitations leading to higher office which allow him to ascend the bureaucratic ladder and start implementing some of his reform ideas, many of which had already been implemented with success in provinces where he had served. There are clear indications in some of his poems that he was waiting for "the right emperor" to ascend the Dragon Throne, which implies his anticipation and understanding of the degree of bureaucratic resistance that would arise against the type of governmental reforms he would promote (see "An Old Pine" #45).

After accepting high office under the reform-minded Emperor Shen Zong, and then leading the reforms that touched virtually every sector of government and society, Wang Anshi was variously described by his contemporaries. An essay entitled "On Discerning Treacherous Officials," traditionally attributed to Su Xun (Su Shi's father and another of the Eight Great Essayists) but probably a forgery, describes Wang as a "tousle-headed and unsavory rascal." Huang Tingjian (Luzhi) describes him as "a famous man of his own day, who regarded wealth and worldly honors as a fleeting cloud, untainted by avarice and lust." (H. R. Williamson, *Wang An Shih, A Chinese Statesman and Educationalist of the Song Dynasty*, II, p98). The scholar, poet, essayist and statesman Su Shi was irreconcilably opposed to Wang's reforms, and yet was a friend and admirer of the man, especially in his later years,

考上进士之后，尚年轻的王安石在京城做了三年的小官。然后，他就不断拒绝得以在官场晋升从而实施他的改革变法的特别的考试，这些变法措施在他工作的各地已实施得很成功。从他的有些诗词中可以看出，他之所以当时不愿出任，是因为他在等候明智的皇帝登上宝座。这表示他了解并预知官场对新的改革之抗拒，所以等候适当的时机以实施和推进他的新法。（参看，第45首《古松》）。

有改革精神的神宗登基之后，王安石接受了高官的职位，因之可以带领实施变法。他的变法影响到政府和社会各个层次。他的影响力不凡，但与他同时代的人有许多对他不同的批判。《辨奸论》一文（传统上认为是苏洵所作，但可能是伪造）称王安石为“囚首丧面，而谈诗书”。黄庭坚在《跋王荆公禅简》中，对王安石的人品十分推崇敬佩：“然余尝熟观其风度，真视富贵如浮云，不溺于财利酒色，一世之伟人也。”苏轼，这一学者、诗人、散文家、政治家，曾积极反对变法，然而却非常敬仰他，也是他的朋友，特别是在他晚年的时候。王安石去世后，苏轼甚至上书请求封他为“太傅”。司马光是王安石政治上最大的对手，而且在神宗去世后撤除王安石所有的变法政策。然而他却称王安石“贤而愎”（《钦定四库全书·御批续资治通鉴纲目》卷六）。朱熹摘引《温公琐语》这样赞赏王安石：“好读书，能强

and even composed the document conferring the honorific title of Grand Tutor on him after his death. Wang's greatest political antagonist, Sima Guang, who dismantled all the reform measures after the death of Emperor Shen Zong, called Wang "a man of highest character, but self-willed." Zhu Xi, whose interpretations of Confucianism became the orthodoxy of succeeding centuries, quoted Sima Guang, who said of him: "He loved to study, and he had a very good memory.... In composing prose, he wielded his pen with flying speed, apparently throwing caution to the winds, but when the piece was finished, all who witnessed it were convinced of his brilliance." (*Complete Works of Zhu Xi*. Shanghai Guji Press, 2010)

记，虽后进投贽及程试文有美者，读一周辄成诵在口，终身不忘。其属文，动笔如飞，初若不措意，文成，见者皆服其精妙。”（《朱子全书》，上海古籍出版社，2010 年版，第 537 页。）

ABOUT WANG ANSHI'S POETRY

Much has been written about Wang Anshi, the man, the statesman, the reformer. We have noted that as an essayist, he is ranked with Han Yu, Liu Zongyuan, Su Shi, etc., as one of the "Eight Great Essayists of the Tang and Song Dynasties." As a poet, he has been acknowledged as one of the all-time masters of the eight-line regulated and quatrain verse forms. About 1,500 of his poems are extant. He composed verse using most of the forms that were popular during his time, but he was at his best when he worked through the eight-line regulated verse and the quatrain verse forms. Since they are widely acknowledged to be his forte, and since the directness of their imagistic communication lends itself well to translation, these shorter poems dominate this collection, although a number of longer verses have been included for two important reasons. First, a few of his most widely anthologized and thus most well-known poems are longer and should therefore be included in any representative collection of his works in translation. Second, some of his most important concerns, ideas, feelings and values – indispensable for a balanced understanding of the man – are best expressed in his longer poems.

Although precise dating is often impossible, most of Wang's extant poems seem to have been written before and after his tenure in highest office, with few written while actually serving

王安石：其诗

有很多文章研究王安石其人、其政治家身份及其变法政策。他的散文也是众所熟知，因为他与韩愈、柳宗元、欧阳修、苏洵、苏轼、苏辙、曾巩合称为“唐宋八大家”。然而，他的诗词却并非人人皆知。但以诗词而论，他是历代以来绝句大家之一。他留给后人的诗词有 1500 首左右。他的诗词包括当时所用的各种诗体，但他最为拿手的是绝句和八行律诗。这些诗是他之所长，而且这些诗里的意象也比较直接和明显，最适合翻译。因之，我们所选出翻译的主要是这些较短的作品，但也有较长的。这有两个原因：首先，因为有些他的较长的诗在很多诗集中出现，比较有名，所以应该包括在翻译集子里；其次，这些较长的诗表现出他关心的事、重要的思想、重要的感情和价值观，是了解他所不可缺少的诗，所以一定要翻译。

我们很难确定他的各首诗词是何时所作，但大多数好像是在他官位最高时之前和之后所作，只有几首是他身为宰相时所作。所以这也是我们不按照他的诗的年代排列的原因之一。我们的排列法力求能表现他的诗词最显著的两点：一是他对于公共和私人最关心的事物；二是他不同程度的觉悟，体现在把他主要关心的事物综合成为那有意义而明智的世界观。

as prime minister. This is one reason why we have attempted to group the poems not chronologically, but in such a manner as to illustrate what we consider to be the two most distinguished aspects of his poetry: his major concerns, both public and private, and his levels of enlightenment revealed in his efforts to integrate his major concerns into a meaningful, enlightened world view.

Like most Chinese poets, Wang composed his verses to commemorate occasions – banquets, festivals, tree plantings, a chat with an old friend, or simply resting alone; he sent poems as letters to friends and relatives; he composed them after naps and in dreams; as games; as inscriptions on temple walls; as criticisms of social injustice; as new works in the persona of ancient poets; as odes in praise of plants and trees as virtuous models for human emulation; in short, he wrote poems to record and give vent to his feelings on a myriad of occasions through his life. By so doing, he observed a great Chinese tradition: "Poetry verbalizes feelings" (shī yán zhì), approaching what we would call the emotional venting function of poetry.

王安石，有如多数的中国诗人，是为纪念不同的场合而作诗，比如：宴请、节庆、植树、与老朋友聊天或者只是休息时。他以诗当信寄给朋友和亲戚；他午睡后和梦中作诗；他把作诗当成游戏；他在寺庙的墙壁上题诗；他为批评社会上不公平的事件或现状作诗；也以古人的身份作新诗；他的诗也歌颂树木和植物为人类模仿的标准。简而言之，他一生中写诗以记录和叙述他对无数场合的情感。因之，他遵守了一项伟大的中国传统，那就是："诗言志。"这就很接近我们所说的：诗的作用是感情的发泄。

The concerns and levels of enlightenment mentioned above, which are the general basis for grouping the 130 poems translated here, are as follows:

(1) Commemorating Occasions, Joyful and Sorrowful.

The joy of reunion, the sorrow of parting (the most common occasions for Chinese occasional poetry).

(2) Sympathy for Suffering People.

The core of Confucianist benevolence (rén), which starts as sympathy, but turns to righteousness (yì) when awareness grows of abuse of power.

(3) Resentment Against Vulgar Powers Who Cause the Suffering of the Poor.

Strength of feeling leads to resentment and cynicism, which gives rise to indignation (yì) at the abuse of power, which in turn engenders ambition to reform (institutionalize fairness and encourage benevolence).

(4) Personal Ambition.

Arising out of a belief that the system may be reformed in such a way as to discourage abuse of power and encourage benevolence.

以上提到的王安石所关心的事物和他觉悟的程度也就是我们将他的130首诗分组的基础。如下：

（1）纪念快活和悲伤的场合。

团圆之乐和离别之悲。

（2）同情受苦难的人。

儒家思想的“仁”，起初是同情，但发现有滥用职权时则变为“义”。

（3）愤恨庸俗的权力，对造成苦难的人之义愤。

强烈的感情使他义愤并玩世不恭，进而产生对腐败权力的义愤，因之引起他变法的雄心，以使事事公平，同时鼓励人人有仁心。

（4）个人的雄心。

此雄心来自一个信念：改变制度即可挫折滥用职权和腐败并鼓励仁心。

(5) Cathartic Self-Pity.

Arising after failure to achieve the noble goals of the reforms.

(6) Mystical Awareness and Appreciation of Non-Ambition and Non-Assertion as Nature's Ideal State.

Achieved through observation and contemplation of nature, and through reading of philosophical poetry such as the Buddhist monk-poet Han Shan's.

(7) Awareness that Even Distinctions between Illusion and Reality are False.

Reality (Truth) is not something that can be defined in words because it is not a thing, but a process that is always in flux.

(8) Being Aware of the Illusory Nature of Human Endeavour, Still Finding It Attractive, and Willing to Live with the Contradiction.

The ultimate stage of "enlightenment" in Wang Anshi's poetry, and perhaps as a philosophy of life. Higher truth is more than the sum of smaller truths that often give the impression of synergy (the whole being greater than the sum of the parts). This conclusion is consistent with the findings of modern Nobel prize-winning physicists.

（5）自怜的发泄。

这种自怜来自变法失败。他对变法有着崇高的目标。

（6）冥冥之中觉悟到并赞赏大自然的另一种状态：无雄心和不勉强。

这是他观察和深思大自然，并且阅读如诗僧寒山的哲学诗词而觉悟到的。

（7）领悟到，甚至幻觉和现实的区别其实也是虚假的。

现实（真理）是不能用语言定名的，因为它不是具体的，而是随时都在变化的。

（8）领悟到，人的努力是幻觉，但仍然感到它有吸引力，因之仍愿意与此矛盾共存。

这是王安石诗词中的至高觉悟，甚至是一个至高的人生哲学。“大真理”大过似是而非的许多“小真理”之和（整体大过组成部分的和）。这一结论是与现代得诺贝尔奖的物理学家的发现吻合的。

Among the eight categories listed above, the first represents the types of occasion-feeling most frequently commemorated in traditional Chinese poetry: the joys of getting together and the sorrows of separation. While we would not argue that the remaining seven categories necessarily represent levels of enlightenment in ascending order, we would suggest that the eighth may indicate the highest level of enlightened understanding: totally accepting both sides of the paradoxical human situation (something akin to accepting Heisenberg's Uncertainty Principle, where human endeavors are particles, history is a wave, and we can't make sense of both at the same time).

以上八项中，第一项代表传统中国诗人经常纪念的各种场合与感情：团圆的喜悦和离别的悲伤。虽然我们不能强调其他七项表现他渐进的悟真程度，但可以说第八项可能表现出他对人类情况觉悟了解的最高程度，那就是：绝对接受自相矛盾的人生情况的两面。（有点像接受海森伯的不定论：人类的努力有如小粒子，历史是海波。我们不能同时理解两者。）

OUR APPROACH TO TRANSLATING THE POEMS

Translation is not only the rendering of words, sentences and longer discourses from one language into another, it is an act of cross-cultural communication, not only crucial for international trade and business negotiations, but also for the enrichment of civilizations. The massive translation of Buddhist sutras from Pali and Sanskrit languages into Chinese had an enormous influence on Chinese culture, and the translation of the same sutras from Chinese into Japanese had similar influence on Japanese culture. Today, in the age of globalization, cross-cultural communication has become an indispensable tool for advancing peaceful, mutually beneficial interaction.

Turning now to poetry, it has been argued that great poetry simply cannot be translated from one language into another, so intimately and inseparably interrelated are the intensive textures of sounds, rhythms and cultural contexts of a great poem. In fact, it has even been suggested, by the poet Robert Frost, that we might define poetry as that which gets lost in translation. He said: "I could define poetry this way: it is that which is lost out of both prose and verse in translation." (Robert Frost, *Conversations on the Craft of Poetry* [1959]). Add to this the Italian adage "traduttore, traditore" ("translator, traitor") and the Hungarian "fordítás: ferdítés" ("translation is distortion"). But Robert Frost also wrote: "[Poetry] is metaphor, saying one thing and meaning another, saying one thing in terms of another, the pleasure of ulteriority.

有关我们的翻译

翻译不是只将字、句或较长的文字从某一语言转到另一种语言，而是一种异文化沟通的行为。翻译不但对国际贸易和商务谈判极为重要，对丰富文明也极为重要。我们知道，大量的佛经从巴利文和梵文翻译成中文对中国文化有着巨大的影响。同时，把佛经从中文翻译成日文对日本文化也起了重大的影响。在今天国际化的时代，异文化沟通已成为促进和平与互利不可缺少的工具。所以翻译也是不可缺少的工具。

就诗词而言，曾有人认为好诗是不能从一种语言翻译成另一种语言的，因为好诗与其声音、韵律和文化内涵有着不可分离的关系。美国诗人罗伯特·弗罗斯特（1874—1963）曾经给诗下定义，他说：“诗是翻译散文和韵文时失去的东西。”（弗罗斯特，1959，《诗的技巧的对话》）。除此之外，还有意大利格言说：“译者，叛者也。”匈牙利有这样的说法：“翻译是扭曲事实。”然而，弗罗斯特也写过：“（诗）是比喻，说此意彼，以此论彼。是一种别有用心的乐趣。诗是以比喻构成的。”（弗罗斯特，1946，《永恒的象征》）既然如此，那翻译的诗不也是一样吗？

Poetry is simply made of metaphor." (Robert Frost, "The Constant Symbol", 1946) If this be true, then may not the same be said of poetry in translation?

The translation of the Hebrew Bible into Greek in the 3rd century BC is seen as the first major work of translation in the Western world, and poetic translations of the *Book of Psalms* have moved readers in countless languages ever since. Translation of foreign poetry into English has been influential for centuries. The sonnet verse form, for example, was non-existent in English until the poet Thomas Wyatt (1503-1542) introduced the sonnet to the English language in the 16th century by translating the works of Petrarch (1304-1374) from Italian. More recently, English translations of Japanese haiku poems have spawned a new English verse form, widely practiced in English and in other languages around the world today.

We prefer to regard the English translation of Chinese poetry as a great challenge to be sure, but no more impossible than the challenge of translating a beautiful and moving psalm from Hebrew or Greek into beautiful, even inspiring English verse. The challenge is to find the right Chinese poem, one relatively unencumbered with allusions that require footnotes to be understood, the right English words as near to the denotative meaning of the original Chinese as smooth and inspired English will allow, and the right versification, preferably retaining similar line length, and using unobtrusive prosodic devices that echo or enhance the sense of the key words and lines in English translation or serve some other supportive function.

公元前三世纪用希腊文翻译希伯来文部分的《圣经》被视为西方首次主要的翻译作品。而且，《圣经》的翻译感动了各种语言的无数读者。许多世纪以来，英文翻译的外国诗都有其深远影响。比如，原先英文里并没有十四行诗。直到十六世纪时，诗人托马斯·怀亚特（1503—1542）将弗朗齐斯克·彼特拉克（1304—1374）的意大利十四行诗翻译成英文，英文的十四行诗才诞生。近年来，英文翻译的日文俳句也产生了一种新的俳句式的诗体，在英文和其他各种语言中广泛应用。

当然我们认为把中文诗词翻译成英文是一种挑战，但是也不会比把感人的希伯来文或希腊文的圣诗翻译成美丽甚至可歌可泣的英文诗更难。挑战性在于选择中文诗，这种诗最好不含有需要太多解释的典故。翻译时用最接近原诗含义的英文、相对的诗律，尽量保持原诗的长短；用合理的诗律法回应或促进原诗重要词语和句子的意义或提供其他附带的功能。

We believe there are basically three types of approach to the English translation of Chinese poetry: the purely didactic, uncompromising focus on the denotative meaning of the words in the original poem; the purely belletristic, uncompromising focus on recreating the moving power of the original poem; and the flexible focus on creating a reaction in the target language reader or listener that comes as close as possible to that of the source language reader or listener, which may be seen as an accommodation of the above two extremes. Our goal in this collection is to produce translated poems that are both creative, in that they involve explorations in English prosody, and re-creative, in that they attempt to reformulate in English the poetic moments once captured by Wang Anshi in a Chinese language and geo-cultural milieu.

Our task has been made easier by the very existence of successful models supplied by other outstanding translator-poets. They have established a workable tradition of translating Chinese verse lines of X character length into English verse lines of X accented or stressed syllables. For example: For "kōng (empty) shān (mountain) bú (not) jiàn (see) rén (person)," we may render it as "The mountains are empty, not a soul is seen" without much damage to the letter or the spirit of the Chinese original, and yet without sacrificing the natural flow of an English utterance.

我们觉得将中文诗词翻译成英文基本上有三种方式：（1）纯教诲式的：注重原诗词语所表现的意思；（2）纯文学式的：注重再创作原诗的感人精神；（3）注重灵活地尽量创造出如原诗一样能感动读者或听众的翻译，是前两种的折中式。我们翻译诗词的目的是希望既有创造性，又有英文诗的诗律，还是再创新：用流畅的英文再造王安石创作时中文和地理文化环境中的诗意。

我们很幸运，因为有卓越的前辈诗人翻译家的很多模式让我们学习。他们建立了一个可行的传统模式，就是可以把中文诗里一行的字数在英文诗的一行里用同样数字的重音来表示。譬如，“空（empty）山（mountain）不（not）见（see）人（person）”，可以翻译成：“The mountains are empty, not a soul is seen”。这样，对原诗的本意和精神并无大碍，同时，英文也算流畅。

On occasion, we have employed such prosodic devices as alliteration and internal rhyme when the repeated sounds serve a structural purpose, such as linking related images or concepts together. For example, the repetition of initials in:

The seasons change so suddenly
the strongest heart is stunned.

时节忽如此，重令壮心惊。
Shí jié hū rú cǐ, chóng lìng zhuàng xīn jīng.

is intended to link the two lines together to recreate the connection of the two Chinese lines.

All of Wang Anshi's Chinese poems employ end rhyme, usually on even-numbered lines, using the same rhyme throughout a single verse. The most successful translators of Chinese poetry in recent decades have avoided end rhyme like the plague, and for good reasons: it usually seems forced and ornamental, detracting from, rather than contributing to, the intensive interrelationship of the poem's meaningful elements. We have employed end rhyme in the last lines of several of our translations, but only under two conditions: when it seemed desirable to reinforce a sense of closure, and when it could be done using natural English word order. For example:

有时，我们也采用头韵或内部押韵，因为重复的音有结构上的作用，比如可以将有关的意象或概念连接在一起。譬如下面的翻译是有意将两行连接起来以表示出原诗的两句：

时节忽如此，重令壮心惊。
The seasons change so suddenly
the strongest heart is stunned.

王安石的诗词都用韵脚，通常是偶数行押韵，全诗用同一韵。近几十年来，成功的翻译家在英文诗里都尽量不在全诗里用韵脚。这是因为通常用韵脚会觉得勉强而不实用，有损于诗意里重要因素的关系。但我们在几首诗中的最后几行用了韵脚，只有两种情况：为了加强结束感和可以用很自然的英文翻译。譬如：

The seasons change so suddenly
the strongest heart is stunned,
and with no one to share their sorrows with mine,
why even bother to pour the wine?

时节忽如此，重令壮心惊。
Shí jié hū rú cǐ, chóng lìng zhuàng xīn jīng.
谅无同忧人，樽酒安可倾。
liàng wú tóng yōu rén, zūn jiǔ ān kě qīng.

Another way of looking at the matter of structure in translation: We try to recreate a natural equivalent to what the Chinese call "qǐ chéng zhuǎn hé" (opening, development, deviation, closure = thesis, antithesis, synthesis) as appropriate to the English language. This involves interplay between visual and conceptual images on the one hand and sounds and rhythms on the other.

时节忽如此，重令壮心惊。

谅无同忧人，樽酒安可倾。

The seasons change so suddenly

the strongest heart is stunned,

and with no one to share their sorrows with mine,

why even bother to pour the wine?

另外一种看翻译中结构的方法是我们在英文翻译中也做到中文里的起承转合（相当于英文里的论点、反论点、综合）。一方面得用视觉和概念意象的互动，另一方面要用声音和韵律的互动。

WANG ANSHI: SELECTED POEMS

POEMS ON OCCASIONS 1-26

I. Conventional Poems with No Criticism of the Political System.

These poems were written to commemorate social and natural events, including the joys of reunion, the sorrows of parting, ritual and festival celebrations, traditionally the most common occasions for writing Chinese poetry.

Most traditional Chinese poetry was composed to commemorate occasions. The most common occasions commemorated include: births, deaths, reunions, farewells, arrivals, departures, outings, visits to historical or beautiful scenic spots, seasonal festivals and signs of a change of season, promotions, banishments, reassignments, battles, famines, dedications, significant dreams, and personal milestones such as noticing one's first grey hair in the mirror. Poems were not composed for publication during Wang's time but were generally composed for recitation at the occasion commemorated – most often to be shared and compared with the poems of colleagues who also composed poems to commemorate the same occasion. Often too, a poem would be sent as a letter to a friend or relative. Poems

王安石：诗选

应景诗 1—26

I. 非政治批评的常规诗

这些诗是为纪念社会和自然事件而作，包括团圆的快乐、离别的悲伤、仪式和节庆的庆祝等最常见的情景。

大多数的古诗都是为应景而作。最普通的是纪念出生、死亡、团圆、告别、抵达、离去、出游、参观历史遗迹或美景、节庆或换季、提升、流放、调动、战役、灾荒、奉献、重要的梦和个人生命中的里程，如初次注意到有白发等。王安石的时代，诗词不是为出版而作的。诗人所作的诗，通常会在某种场合吟诵，而且也常与同时写诗的朋友交换和比较各自的诗。诗作也常像信件一样送给亲友。这一组诗也

in this category illustrate a significant key to understanding Wang's sensibilities: even his poems celebrating fundamentally auspicious events or occasions may be tinged with sad or melancholy awareness of the ultimate futility awaiting the happiest endeavors. His sensitivity to, and acceptance of, the principle of irony underlies his keenest insights into the human situation.

是为了解王安石感性的关键诗：他庆祝最吉利的喜庆的事也会带着一点悲伤的阴影，在最快活的时节，他也会觉悟到最终还是一场空而已。他对绝妙的讽刺性的感受和认可是他对人世最敏锐的洞察。

- 1 -

NEW YEAR'S DAY

A whole year blown away
by the firecrackers' boom,
a spring breeze brings warmth
into fresh wine.

Sunshine glows on the gates
of thousands of homes
as people take down old door charms
and put up the new.

元日*

爆竹声中一岁除，春风送暖入屠苏。
千门万户曈曈日，总把新桃换旧符。

* 本书中文版诗词参照版本：《临川先生文集》，中华书局（香港分局），1971 年 8 月。

- 2 -

QING MING

The drinking ended on the east side of town,
the sun sets slow,
in southern fields a swing dangles
empty, alone.

Someone lies on fragrant grass
with a tall jug
as winds whistle through green twigs
like high-pitched pipes.

清明

东城酒散夕阳迟，南陌秋千寂寞垂。
人与长瓶卧芳草，风将急管度青枝。

- 3 -

AN INVITATION TO LÜ JIAWEN

It occurs to me that you'll be on the move,
so I invite you to come to my home.

We'll draw water from my mountainside spring,
cook my vegetables, all garden-grown.

I know you have a humane heart
that could not bear to hook my fish,
my pond is in a humane realm
where otters do not prey,
nor will you find maggots here
groping for garbage everywhere.

After we dine, we'll stroll and enjoy the view:
fish will swish the algae and the rush,
ripples glowing in the white sunlight
as tails wiggle and whiskers wave,
and don't think this joy is just for fish
with none for you and me.

We'll play and sing of golden days,
finding pleasure in these ways.

要望之过我庐

念子且行矣，要子过我庐。
汲我山下泉，煮我园中蔬。
知子有仁心，不忍钓我鱼。
我池在人境，不与獱獭居。
亦复无虫蛆，出没争腐余。
食罢往游观，鲅鲅藻与蒲。
清波映白日，摆尾扬其须。
岂鱼有此乐，而我与子无。
击壤谣圣时，自得以为娱。

- 4 -

OLD TREE

Last year, when the north wind blew
cracks in the roof tiles,
the old tree by the wall
froze until it nearly split.

Green leaves now shade the house
as suddenly it flourishes again:
now the wild birds
find it livable once more,

and soon there will be countless
sounds of bird calls
as male and female all
sing in tune.

I thumb through books in bed
for my noonday nap,
but they arouse me
with their chattering.

In an old poem a bird call
deepens the mountain's mystique,
but not so deep, I feel,
as when the calling has stopped.

I only dread the day
when this will cease to be
and raging winds will come again
to abuse the old tree.

老树

去年北风吹瓦裂，墙头老树冻欲折。
苍叶蔽屈忽扶疏，野禽从此相与居。
禽鸣无时不可数，雌雄各自应律吕。
我床拨书当午眠，能惊我眠聒我语。
古诗鸟鸣山更幽，我念不若鸣声收。
但忧此物一朝去，狂风还来欺老树。

- 5 -

PLUM BLOSSOMS

Wind and snow blow at year's end
even down south,
where red plum blossoms also
spread the news of spring.

Their color in the cruel cold
is pale from start to end,
drawing sorrow even before
the withering begins.

江梅

江南岁尽多风雪，也有红梅漏泄春。
颜色凌寒终惨澹，不应摇落始愁人。

- 6 -

THE TAOIST MASTER OF NORTH MOUNTAIN PLANTING PINE TREES

Snow starts melting in the warm breeze
on sun-drenched slopes,
as far as you can see around the valley
things are growing green.

May your pine trees prosper and grow
until they brush the skies,
and may you return in a later life
to hear the temple bell toll.

北山道人栽松

阳坡风暖雪初融，度谷遥看积翠重。
磊砢拂天吾所爱，他生来此听楼钟。

- 7 -

VIEWING THE MOON WITH A FRIEND ON MID-AUTUMN FESTIVAL NIGHT

Oceanic mists bathe the eye
as the autumn sun fades from sight.

So bright! I wonder how it can be night.
So clear! The earth seems to disappear.

We sit before the sweeping breeze
linger with cups while the dew congeals.

We'll moan our mournful songs till dawn,
and how can there be any thought of a "me"?

陪友人中秋夕赏月

海雾看如洗，秋阳望却昏。
光明疑不夜，清莹欲无坤。
扫掠风前坐，留连露下尊。
苦吟应到晓，况有我思存。

\- 8 -

ON MEETING AND FAREWELL ARBOR

West City Road
where residents bid travelers
farewell as they head west.

Year after year we wonder
when will our turn come?
and another boat today
is on its way.

Spring breezes blow blossoms
down from the highest limbs,
fluttering here and there,
never aware.

Travelers on the road
are really like this too,
for there will come a day
when they are sent away.

书会别亭

西城路，居人送客西归处。
年年借问去何时，今日扁舟从此去。
春风吹花落高枝，飞来飞去不自知。
路上行人亦如此，应有重来此处时。

- 9 -

ON THE YANGTZE

River waters shiver in the west wind,
river blossoms shed their late red.

Separation's sorrow is blown from a flute
over the jumbled hills to the east.

江上

江水漾西风，江花脱晚红。
离情被横笛，吹过乱山东。

- 10 -

ANCHORING AT GUAZHOU

From Jingkou to Guazhou
there's only a river's length,
and Mount Zhong is just
a few hills away.

A spring breeze greens
the shores down south;
this brilliant moon, I wonder when
it will light my way home again?

泊船瓜洲

京口瓜洲一水间，钟山只隔数重山。
春风又绿江南岸，明月何时照我还。

- 11 -

AT JIAKOU IN JIANGNING
(Third of three poems)

I lower sail at the river's mouth
under a pale moon,
over there is a lampless inn,
just about to close.

A half-dead maple leans
over the sandy shore,
and tying the boat, I seem to see
scars from years before.

江宁夹口三首（其三）

落帆江口月黄昏，小店无灯欲闭门。
侧出岸沙枫半死，系船应有去年痕。

- 12 -

ANOTHER INSCRIPTION FOR SOUTH BROOK PAVILION

Billowing clouds above North Mountain,
ever flowing waters of South Brook;
leaving here was not my idea,
before we go, I come up for one last look.

再题南涧楼

北山云漠漠，南涧水悠悠。
去此非吾愿，临分更上楼。

- 13 -

SENDING OFF GENG TIANZHI AT THE FERRY CROSSING

Snow clouds hover above the river
yet we chatter on and on,
for unlike any other time
we grieve at this parting of ways.

Our minds have worked as one
while forty years passed by;
few are the friends that ever have been
as close as you and I.

送耿天骘至渡口

雪云江上语依依，不比寻常恨有违。
四十余年心莫逆，故人如我与君稀。

- 14 -

TO CHEN XUANSHU

My little boat was about to move on,
then hesitated again
as the mere sight of your smile
kept my weary eyes wide.

The powers that be finally see
your integrity,
and governments in thriving counties
all proclaim your genius.

I was shaken to see how time had taken
such a toll on the brow,
but still rejoiced to share a cup
with you by the mountain stream.

Drifting aimlessly under the setting sun,
as I head up north,
this far away heart, like the stream,
flows back east to you.

寄陈宣叔

扁舟欲动更徘徊，一笑相看病眼开。
事忤贵人今见节，政行豪县众称材。
忽惊岁月侵双鬓，却喜山川共一杯。
落日乱流江北去，离心犹与水东回。

- 15 -

TO MY ELDEST DAUGHTER, MRS. WU, AFTER ENCOUNTERING A SHOWER WHEN SEEING MY BROTHER ANLI OFF TO LONG'AN

Boundless mist and cool rain
goad a person's grief
as tears stain our gowns
totally unaware.

Except for the spring breeze
and the green on the sandy shore,
everything is now as it was then
when I watched you cross the ford.

送和甫至龙安微雨因寄吴氏女子

荒烟凉雨助人悲，泪染衣襟不自知。
除却春风沙际绿，一如看汝过江时。

- 16 -

ORALLY COMPOSED ON THE MOLING ROAD
(Second of two poems)

Farmers rejoice, for crops are ripe,
but the traveler grieves alone in the autumn wind.

This road to Qucheng winds on and on,
and a horse heads homeward in the setting sun.

秣陵道中口占二首（其二）

岁熟田家乐，秋风客自悲。
茫茫曲城路，归马日斜时。

- 17 -

TO A FRIEND

A drifting traveler on a road
with no end in sight,
a long look southwestward
brings a hundred sighs.

The river pushes streams of tears
flowing out to sea,
winds blow a dreaming soul
all the way home.

I've gathered a whole life of grief,
enough to dissolve my bones,
and now today I'm watching blossoms
bloom in another land.

If only I could find a way to live
like the grass and trees,
I'd be spending all my years
tending to my roots.

寄友人

飘然羁旅尚无涯，一望西南百叹嗟。
江拥涕洟流入海，风吹魂梦去还家。
平生积惨应销骨，今日殊乡又见花。
安得此身如草树，根株相守尽年华。

- 18 -

COMPOSED ON HORSEBACK, RETURNING FROM LAKEVIEW PAVILION OF HANGZHOU
Presented to Yuru and Ledao

Water's glow and mountain mist
floating in the green,
at sunset we start to leave,
then linger longer still.

Hereafter this can only enter
into my dreams,
for there I still can enjoy myself
with my old friends.

杭州望湖楼回马上作呈玉汝乐道

水光山气碧浮浮，落日将归又少留。
从此只应长入梦，梦中还与故人游。

- 19 -

IN MEMORY OF WANG FENGYUAN*

Since I lost Fengyuan
everything makes me grieve,
not just because he was an old friend,
truly I mourn as though for myself.

Who knew me when I was at my best?
and who was aware of my every fault?
Who came to think and plan with me?
and who was there to listen when I spoke?

Off at dawn, we shared a single horse,
and on a single horse returned at night.
Racing and running and getting nowhere,
we chatted and laughed and made the most of it.

Now lying in my room, I can only sigh,
or walking about, I weep,
thinking of your grave mound
and how only weeds now grow on that ground.

Such a lovely wife, and still so young,
a widow now, living alone.
Her honor has stirred the neighborhood
to share their wealth with her.

* Wang Fengyuan: Wang Ling (1032-1059).

思王逢原

自吾失逢原，触事辄愁思。
岂独为故人，抚心良自悲。
我善孰相我，孰知我瑕疵。
我思谁能谋，我语听者谁。
朝出一马驱，暝归一马驰。
驰驱不自得，谈笑强追随。
仰屋卧太息，起行涕淋漓。
念子冢上土，草茅已纷披。
婉婉妇且少，茕茕一女嫠。
高义动闾里，尚闻致财赀。

Alas, I who only serve at court
can barely offer her a bit of porridge.
Unable to help with the funeral at all,
what use is my grief-torn face?

I hear that she may come back up north,
and I watch and wait for her return.
The chill River Bian is already sealed,
which means a treacherous trip,
and they say that she is with child,
a child to be born at an unknown time.
A good man's family should endure,
and I know she must "dream of bears." *

Heaven can be trusted no more,
our hope lies here alone.
I am worn out, my writings misconstrued,
out of tune with the rest of the world.

Long ago together we planned
to thatch our huts upon the same hill,
but that affair is finished now,
finished, and known to none.

So deep are the rivers and lakes,
so vast the mountains and crags,
how can one eat food unearned
after failing commitments to a friend?

* "Dream of bears": alludes to a poem in the *Book of Songs* (*Shi Jing*), in which it augurs the birth of a male heir.

嗟我衣冠朝，略能具饘糜。
葬祭无所助，哀颜亦何施。
闻妇欲北返，跂予常望之。
寒汴已闭口，此行又参差。
又说当产子，产子知何时。
贤者宜有后，固当梦熊罴。
天方不可恃，我愿适在兹。
我疲学更误，与世不相宜。
宿昔心已许，同冈结茅茨。
此事今已矣，已矣尚谁知。
渺渺江与潭，茫茫山与陂。
安能久窃食，终负故人期。

- 20 -

SPRING DAY

Spring moves slowly on to dusk
as things race to bloom everywhere.

The oriole still seeks out old friends
and swallows return even to a poor home.

I have the wine of sages in the house
but no important carriages at my door.

Drunk, I can sleep without explaining why
and return, in dreams, to the rim of the sky.

春日

冉冉春行暮，菲菲物竞华。
莺犹求旧友，雁不背贫家。
室有贤人酒，门无长者车。
醉眠聊自适，归梦到天涯。

- 21 -

A NAP

I nap among so many blossoms
my mat almost floats away
while the sun chases colorful shadows
up to the curtain hook.

A peeping bird calls
to my gracefully drifting dream
a sweet and subtle sadness fed
by mountains beyond the stream.

午枕

午枕花前簟欲流，日催红影上帘钩。
窥人鸟唤悠扬梦，隔水山供宛转愁。

- 22 -

RETURNING HOME

Wouldn't it be wonderful to be back home!
but the business of life gives me no idle time.

The morning sun has risen again
and I'm back on the saddle once more.

Sadness flows in a hundred streams
and a million mountains block my view.

How to forget this bridled roaming?
by staying carefree in drunken dreams.

还家

还家岂不乐，生事未应闲。
朝日已复出，征鞍方更攀。
伤心百道水，阂目万重山。
何以忘羁旅，翛然醉梦间。

- 23 -

HOME IN ONE DAY
(Mourning the Death of My Wife)

In poverty, I race about
for our food and clothes,
a hundred days of scurrying,
now home in one day.

We were happy with our life
of endless suffering
and we were just about to spend
old age in each other's arms.

Her empty room feels so bleak
when funeral curtains hang,
by an old lamp at midnight
whimpering grows faint.

Her voice and face stay on my mind
wherever she may go,
I can only hope to pay her back
when we meet down below.

一日归行

贱贫奔走食与衣，百日奔走一日归。
平生欢意苦不尽，正欲老大相因依。
空房萧瑟施穗帷，青灯半夜哭声稀。
音容想像今何处，地下相逢果是非。

- 24 -

READING ABOARD A BOAT

We pass beneath slowly falling leaves
as the autumn landscape grows more bleak.
Fields and plains carry drifting clouds,
the setting sun hugs a sandbar.

I step inside, but find no one to chat with,
go out on deck, find nothing worth the search,
so, since their inspiration always has me in hold,
I decide to consult the great writers of old.

舟中读书

冉冉木叶下，萧萧山水秋。
浮云带田野，落日抱汀洲。
归卧无与语，出门何所求。
未能忘感慨，聊以古人谋。

- 25 -

AUTUMNAL MOOD

The flatlands south of town
are cold and covered with frost.
Windows swallow the wind
as airs of autumn arrive.

Mulberry trees next door so sparse
they're nearly bare,
grieving insects wail and cry,
speeding the shuttle through the loom.

Thatch door half shut,
I sweep bird tracks away
and carry a stack of tattered old books
to a meeting with the gods!

Han Yu is already long gone,
no sense in chasing him,
but if Mencius should happen by today
I wouldn't turn him away.

秋怀

城南平野寒多露，窗壁含风秋气度。
邻桑槭槭已欲空，悲虫啾啾促机杼。
柴门半掩扫鸟迹，独抱残编与神遇。
韩公既去岂能追，孟子有来还不拒。

- 26 -

SENDING OFF XIE SHIZAI TO SERVE IN CHUZHOU (Second of two poems)

The long stream flows eastward
all the way from Mt. Kunlun,
and boats move along it
like brisk autumn winds.

I'm glad you can have this happy trip
while you're still so young and strong,
too bad I must stay behind,
nothing to do but grow old.

By the shores of the river
the water flows on and on
as we lean on the railing
watching lotus blossoms spread red.

The time may come when you and I
can no longer clasp hands,
but today, at least, our eyes are filled
only with hills and streams.

送谢师宰赴任楚州（其二）

昆仑一支流向东，七月八月船如风。
爱君少壮此行乐，恨我留连成老翁。
神头两岸水无穷，伏槛荷花满地红。
当时不得君携手，今日山川在眼中。

SYMPATHY 27-31

II. Expressing Sympathy for People Who Suffer under Systemic Abuse.

This is the core idea of Confucianist benevolence (rén): moved by humane sympathy, Wang's growing awareness of systemic abuse channels his feelings toward resentment. Like most civilized Chinese of his time, Wang was taught to believe that all human beings are basically similar in nature, inherently good at birth, but that subsequent differences in life experience condition differences in character. He believed that the noblest guide for human behavior may be summarized with the word benevolence (rén), of which Confucius himself had this to say: "Benevolent people, wishing to establish themselves, seek also to establish others; wishing to perfect themselves, they seek also to perfect others." (*Analects of Confucius*, Yong ye, #30). At its gentlest, Wang's benevolence is manifest in such poems as "On Setting a Fish Free" (#27). Sympathy on the verge of righteous indignation is revealed in such verses as "Moved by Events" (#31).

王安石：诗选

同情心 27—31

II. 抒发对受腐败政策之害的苦难的人之同情心

这是儒家思想“仁”的中心思想：被同情心感动，王安石越来越感悟到政策的腐败，甚至变为愤怒。一如与他同时期的有知识的人，他相信人之初性本善；人因为生活经验的不同而产生不同的性格。他认为指引最高尚行为的可以总结为“仁”。孔子说：“己欲立而立人，己欲达而达人。”（《论语·雍也》，30）。王安石最慈善时的仁心表现在如《放鱼》（27）诗中。他的同情心的义愤表现在如《感事》（31）诗中。

- 27 -

ON SETTING A FISH FREE

I caught a fish in the shallows of a stream
and tossed him back into the deepest part.
Having beat the heat of cooking fires,
gracefully, he swam away.

Not that we have no good cook
to turn him into a gourmet dish,
but all of us dread suffering, and so
I dine on vegetables and let him go.

放鱼

捉鱼浅水中，投置最深处。
当暑脱煎熬，翛然泳而去。
岂无良庖者，可使供匕箸。
物我皆畏苦，舍之宁啖茹。

- 28 -

FIFTEEN VERSES RHYMING WITH MEI SHENGYU'S* "POEMS ON OBJECTS AROUND THE FARM" (First of 15 poems)

THE HUT BY THE FIELD

A farmer builds a hut by his field,
big enough to hold him when he rests,
calls his son to fetch bamboo and straw,
never leans on his neighbor for help.

He rises and leaves the hut at dawn,
returns to sleep in the hut at night,
and so it goes, different ways for all –
don't laugh at the field hut for being small.

* Mei Shengyu: The famous Song poet Mei Yaochen (1002-1060).

和圣俞农具诗十五首

其一 田庐

田父结田庐，聊容一身息。
呼儿取茅竹，不借乡人力。
起行庐旁朝，归卧庐下夕。
悠悠各有愿，勿笑田庐窄。

- 29 -

FINE JADE

A fine piece of jade with a little flaw
is still prized by the State Artisan,
and a worthy man with a shortcoming
isn't cast aside by his friends.

Shortcomings can be patched
as we polish little flaws.
Polishing and patching: without these two,
what can people do about you?

美玉

美玉小瑕疵，国工犹珍之。
大贤小玷缺，良交岂其绝。
小缺可以补，小瑕可以磨。
不补亦不磨，人为奈尔何。

- 30 -

THE HEBEI FOLK

Oh, the Hebei folk!
Life on the frontier
is forever hard:

Families raise their young
to learn to plow and weave,
then give them to the government
to serve in barbarian wars.

This year there is a great drought
and thousands of miles are scorched,
but the counties are still made
to find forced labor for the River,
so young and old, hand in hand,
migrate to the south,
where even in the best of times
folks can't feed themselves.

Sadness darkens
the world at midday,
passers-by along the road
are gaunt.

Better to have lived
in High Tang times
when a few coins could buy a bushel of rice
and there were no wars!

河北民

河北民，生近二边长苦辛。
家家养子学耕织，输与官家事夷狄。
今年大旱千里赤，州县仍催给河役。
老小相携来就南，南人丰年自无食。
悲愁白日天地昏，路旁过者无颜色。
汝生不及贞观中，斗粟数钱无兵戎。

- 31 -

MOVED BY EVENTS

Long ago, before I was in office,
my heart would grieve for the common folk.

In the best of years they never eat their fill,
how much less their lot in flood or drought?

Although no robbers rampage now,
chances are that soon they will.

Officials are dreaded worst of all –
they bring disaster to nine homes in ten.

When millet and wheat have failed in the fields
folks can't afford the bribes to appeal for relief.

If at last they are "blessed" with an inspection tour
the whipping cane follows close behind.

Worst of all, between winter and spring,
the old and the weak die stiff.

感事

贱子昔在野，心哀此黔首。
丰年不饱食，水旱尚何有。
虽无剽盗起，万一且不久。
特愁吏之为，十室灾八九。
原田败粟麦，欲诉嗟无赇。
间关幸见省，笞扑随其后。
况是交冬春，老弱就僵仆。

The prefect seals the granaries
and deputies press for debts with whips.

The villagers stripped of their last possessions,
their men arrested, their fields lie bare.

But the state receives just a fraction of the loot
while devious scoundrels grow rich.

And all along those fools rest content
who call themselves "The Guardian of the Folk"!

Since coming to aid in this poor district's rule
I shudder with fear and hurt inside,
for now I am the one in charge of the wrongs
that pained my heart long ago!

The Sage himself could hardly run the farms,
how much less the likes of me!

I must spur myself to do my very best
and, working with my fellows in office, never rest!

州家闭仓庾，县吏鞭租负。
乡邻铢两徵，坐逮空南亩。
取赀官一毫，奸桀已云富。
彼昏方怡然，自谓民父母。
朅来佐荒郡，懔懔常惭疚。
昔之心所哀，今也执其咎。
乘田圣所勉，况乃余之陋。
内讼敢不勤，同忧在僚友。

RESENTMENT 32-42

III. Resentment Against Vulgar Powers, and Indignation Against Those Who Cause Suffering through Systemic Abuse.

Wang's strength of commitment to benevolence (rén) leads to resentment, which in turn gives rise to abuse of power, which in turn engenders ambition to reform: do away with the abuses that cause the system to fall short.

Were there no heartfelt commitment to benevolence, there would be no resentment and indignation at unjust treatment of others. Sincere commitment to benevolence, however, leads inevitably to indignation, and awareness of the latter calls either for action to rectify injustice, or for the hypocritical turning of a blind eye toward it. In many of his poems, Wang appears genuinely committed to the principle of benevolence as the cornerstone of civilization, shows indignation in the face of injustice, and instinctively would act to bring about rectification. He is aware that most gentlemen, preferring not to rock the boat, would prefer turning the blind eye, as revealed in the poem "We Feast in the Hall at Sunrise" (#36). Similar feelings of undisguised resentment, contempt and disdain for systemic abuse are revealed in "Land Grabbing" (#34) and "Confiscating Salt" (#35).

王安石：诗选

愤慨 32—42

III. 愤恨庸俗的权力，义愤由腐败的政策造成的苦难

王安石强烈的对“仁”的信服引起他的愤慨，因之产生对滥用政权的义愤，使变法的雄心油然而生，以排除滥用政权的情况。

如果没有全心全意信服“仁”，则不会有对不公平对待别人情况的愤慨和义愤。前者诚意的信服就不可避免地引致后者。对后者的信服就会使之采取行动，矫正不公平。不然，只好盲目无视。在他相当多的诗里，王安石真心信服仁道为文明的基石。一发现有不公平的事，他就会表现义愤，并本能地采取行动以矫正之。他很清楚多数人不愿无事生非，宁可盲目无视，正如他的诗《日出堂上饮》（36）所记。有如这样的、明显的对腐败政策的愤慨、蔑视和鄙弃也表现在《兼并》（34）和《收盐》（35）诗中。

- 32 -

IN PRAISE OF THE MOON

Trailing behind the sunken sun
it dies to be born again,
decorating the drifting clouds,
now pale, now bright.

But with rivers full of flood dragons
and wild beasts roaming the hills,
I wouldn't dare to wander there
even in broad daylight.

咏月

追随落日尽还生，点缀浮云暗又明。
江有蛟龙山虎豹，清光虽在不堪行。

- 33 -

COUNTRYSIDE STROLL

Tender mulberry leaves picked so clean
green and shade are sparse
while silkworms in reed-beds
grow fat inside cocoons.

I chat with a villager
about local lore
and why, after all their hard work,
they are starving as before.

郊行

柔桑采尽绿阴稀，芦箔蚕成密茧肥。
聊向村家问风俗：如何勤苦尚凶饥？

- 34 -

LAND GRABBING

In the Golden Age, the common folk were loved like sons,
all wealth was either public or their own.

Sovereigns held the reins of rule
like the North Star holds the Dipper.

Give and take determined by the throne,
land grabbing was wickedly viewed.

The wicked were punished by the Law,
no way for their likes to gain sway.

Then later, things were turned around
and control of the people was lost.

The First Emperor of Qin, unaware of this,
built a memorial to chaste widows.

兼并

三代予百姓，公私无异财。
人主擅操柄，如天持斗魁。
赋予皆自我，兼并乃奸回。
奸回法有诛，势亦无自来。
后世始倒持，黔首遂难裁。
秦王不知此，更筑怀清台。

The values of old faded away, day by day,
the works of the Sages buried in the dust of ages.

The letter of the Law is still around
but those who would apply it are scorned.

Vulgar officials know no right –
their only genius is the squeeze;
vulgar scholars brook no change:
"Abolish land grabbing? What for?"

So many loopholes for private gain
by petty men with selfish schemes
while those in power struggle with each other –
tough luck for the miserable folk!

礼义日已偷，圣经久堙埃。
法尚有存者，欲言时所咍。
俗吏不知方，掊克乃为材。
俗儒不知变，兼并可无摧。
利孔至百出，小人私阖开。
有司与之争，民愈可怜哉。

- 35 -

CONFISCATING SALT*

Orders fly from the prefecture
thicker than the teeth of a comb
making confiscation of salt from the sea
even tighter than before.

Wretched 'criminals' huddling in hovels
can do nothing but sigh
as officers with arms patrol
back and forth in their boats.

All these islands in the sea
have been barren for ages,
and now the wretched islanders
are even harder pressed.

If they can't distill salt from the sea
they're sure to starve to death.
How could they go on suffering like this,
never to break away?

They are driven to piracy now,
roaming everywhere,
plundering and murdering merchants,
sinking their ships.

"The welfare of the populace
is our prime concern."
How, then, can these 'gentlemen' bear
to grapple for their crumbs?

* During Wang's time as a young official, production and selling of salt was a government monopoly.

收盐

州家飞符来比栉，海中收盐今复密。
穷囚破屋正嗟郗，吏兵操舟去复出。
海中诸岛古不毛，岛夷为生今独劳。
不煎海水饿死耳，谁肯坐守无亡逃。
尔来贼盗往往有，劫杀贾客沈其艘。
一民之生重天下，君子忍与争秋毫。

- 36 -

WE FEAST IN THE HALL AT SUNRISE

We feast in the hall at sunrise
with no talk of stopping at dusk.
Our host is smiling through his songs
while guests sigh and complexions change.

See that pillar in the hall?
It used to live high on a secluded cliff
bathed in the rain and by the dew,
it towered through the clouds for a thousand years
looking forward to eternity.

Then by chance it was chosen for our lord
and ordered to descend into dank lowlands
where hordes of termites ate its heart away.
Now hollow decoration for appearances alone,
it can hardly bear its burden from above.

日出堂上饮

日出堂上饮，日西未云休。
主人笑而歌，客子叹以愀。
指此堂上柱，始生在岩幽。
雨露饱所滋，凌云亦千秋。
所托愿求久，何言值君收。
乃令卑湿地，百蚁上穷锼。
丹青空外好，镇压已堪忧。

For the sake of our lord I would drive them all away,
allowing not one termite to remain!
for though one termite may be weak
one may breed a million of its kind
and once again their base will grow:
either they die, or they multiply.

Don't be so concerned, the guests are told,
your hundred years are a bubble on the sea.
Good guests need only offer good toasts –
why get involved with schemes for the host?

为君重去之，不使一蚁留。
蚁力虽云小，能生万蚍蜉。
又能高其础，不尔继者稠。
语客且勿然，百年等浮沤。
为客当酌酒，何豫主人谋。

- 37 -

SHANG YANG*

People are always guided
by trust and honesty,
a word, once given, should weigh more
than a hundred nuggets of gold.

People today really shouldn't
censure Shang Yang –
Shang Yang knew what law was about:
the laws he laid down were always carried out!

商鞅

自古驱民在信诚，一言为重百金轻。
今人未可非商鞅，商鞅能令政必行。

* Shang Yang was Prime Minister of Qin during the fourth century B.C. Known as a Legalist, his strict administration of the Legalist system of rewards and punishments contributed to the strengthening of Qin. Ironically, he died by execution, a victim of the very laws he had promulgated.

- 38 -

JIA YI

This Luoyang lad in Han times
knew right from wrong even as a child.

Every word he uttered was inspired,
and believing in himself, he never went astray.

But if the dead could come to life again
who would he follow today?

He'd drown himself in the Eastern Sea
and not just soak his sleeves in tears.

贾生

汉有洛阳子，少年明是非。
所论多感概，自信肯依违。
死者若可作，今人谁与归。
应须蹈东海，不但涕沾衣。

- 39 -

WHILE SERVING IN SHUZHOU
On the Occasion of Turning Down the Invitation to Take the Advanced Placement Examinations

You can't look up to heaven
with a basin on your head.
How I blame empty fame,
how I detest it!

Coarse food and ritual feasts
both have their allure
but maybe the earthworm alone
is clean and pure!

舒州被召试不赴偶书

戴盆难与望天兼，自怪虚名亦自嫌。
槁壤太牢俱有味，可能蚯蚓独清廉。

- 40 -

**WRITTEN IN JEST
ON SEEING A PARROT**

When will those wings drum again
among the trees and clouds?
Jade cage and gold lock
hold resentment alone.

Nothing to do but struggle
to learn human words,
for no one in the human world
will understand birds.

见鹦鹉戏作四句

云木何时两翅翻，玉笼金锁只烦冤。
真须强学人间语，举世无人解鸟言。

- 41 -

BLOSSOMING PLUM
ON SOLITARY MOUNTAIN

What can you compare it to,
this Solitary Mountain plum?

Right between bloom and fade
in the midst of thorns,
a discarded lover
left to the bush and trees,
a frustrated loyal statesman
staying in the weeds.

Straight and tall, in lone splendor
it stands in the winter sun,
silent, still, its subtle fragrance
follows the wind in the wilds.

Its roots have taken hold now,
too late to be moved away –
Looking back on Imperial Gardens,
how bland they seem today.

独山梅花

独山梅花何所似，半开半谢荆棘中。
美人零落依草木，志士憔悴守蒿蓬。
亭亭孤艳带寒日，漠漠远香随野风。
移栽不得根欲老，回首上林颜色空。

- 42 -

TO ZENG ZIGU*

I'm ashamed that my little ration
affords such a petty gift
and I regret that this path of mine
is so hard to pave.

I'd rather be free from groveling for grain
and give rein to my will,
but wear myself out serving the people,
though not to gain fame.

So many times degenerates
have scrapped high ideals,
heroic dreams seldom meet
with the care of an old friend.

I look back toward the wasted town
but hills and streams are in the way,
and feel how the autumn winds blow,
and the white hairs grow.

* Zeng Gong (1019-1083), one of the "Eight Great Essayists of the Tang and Song Dynasties.

寄曾子固

斗粟犹惭报礼轻，敢嗟吾道独难行。
脱身负米将求志，戮力乘田岂为名。
高论几为衰俗废，壮怀难值故人倾。
荒城回首山川隔，更觉秋风白发生。

WANG ANSHI: SELECTED POEMS

AMBITION 43-49

IV. Revealing Ambition to Reform.

These poems show Wang's belief that the system could be reformed in such a way as to discourage abuse and encourage benevolence. His attempts to reform the system, however, were resisted by conservative idealists as well as by beneficiaries of the old system with all its injustices. Conservative resistance eventually succeeded and led Wang the reformer predictably to disappointment and self-pity.

Wang Anshi believed in the possibility, desirability and rightness of the reforms, that is, the "New Laws" (xīnfǎ), for which he became both famous and infamous. Yet he did not rush to take advantage of the first several opportunities – virtual invitations – to move to the capital and begin introducing on a national scale the reforms he had implemented with noted success in the field. In his writings he shows his awareness that everything depends upon choosing the right time under the right conditions. His high ambition, his firm sense of self-confidence and his knowledge of the importance of timing and conditions, including support by the right Emperor, are revealed in several poems, as in "An Old Pine" (#45) and "Parasol Tree in the Autumn Sun" (#48).

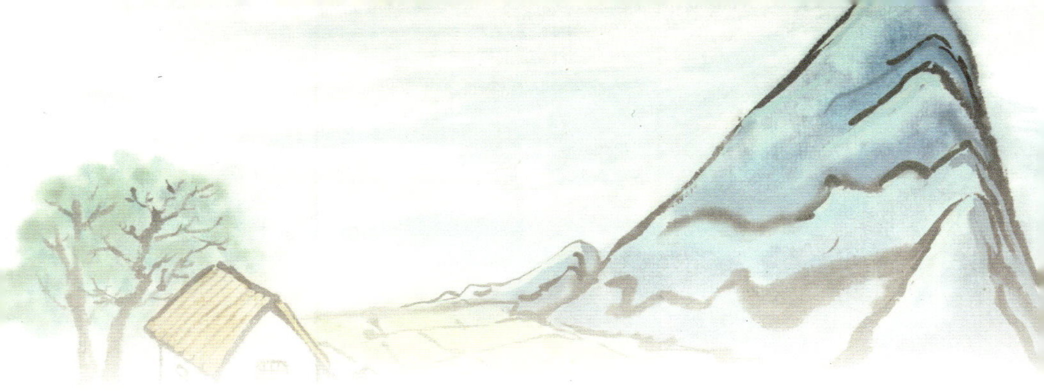

王安石：诗选

雄心 43—49

Ⅳ. 显现变法的雄心

王安石的这些诗显示出他相信更新政策可以阻止腐败而鼓励仁心。然而，他的变法遭到保守派的反抗，同时也受到腐败政策受惠者的反抗。最后，保守派的反抗得以成功。可想而知，这使变法者王安石大为失望并自怜。

王安石相信改革的需要、可行性和正确性。他终于因新法而有名，也因之而毁誉。然而，这也是因为他没有利用最初被邀请去都城做官的机会。不然，他早已可以开始在全国推行在地方上已相当成功的新法。在他的写作里，他表现出觉察到什么事都取决于时间和条件。他在好几首诗里都显示出雄心、绝对的信心，显示出了解时间和条件以及明君支持的重要性。如：《古松》（45）和《秋日在梧桐》（48）。

- 43 -

XIE AN HILL*
(First of two poems)

My name and your nickname
happen to be the same,
and from my house your hill
is in full view,

but you are gone and I have come,
the hill belongs to me –
no reason why the hill should still
be named after thee!

谢安墩二首（其一）

我名公字偶相同，我屋公墩在眼中。
公去我来墩属我，不应墩姓尚随公。

* Xie An (320-385), also known as Xie Anshi, was an important minister during the Jin Dynasty. The hill which bears his name is in the northern part of today's Nanjing.

- 44 -

ON CLIMBING MOUNT FLEW-IN

A thousand-yard high pagoda
stands on Flew-in Peak.
Legend says at cock's crow
you can see to the very sunrise.

No need to worry that floating clouds
may block the longer view,
for I am now standing tall
on the highest peak of all.

登飞来峰

飞来山上千寻塔，闻说鸡鸣见日升。
不畏浮云遮望眼，自缘身在最高层。

- 45 -

AN OLD PINE

The tall straight trunk soars
a hundred rods and more
up into blue heights
where no forest can lay claim.

Winds born of myriad valleys
become its voice in the night,
the moon shining on a thousand hills
hangs in its autumn shade.

Such strength didn't come
from nurturing with night soil,
but was created by the kindness
of Heaven, Earth and Nature.

The court that needs quality
would do well to take it,
but without a good carpenter
the world had best forsake it.

古松

森森直干百余寻，高入青冥不附林。
万壑风生成夜响，千山月照挂秋阴。
岂因粪壤栽培力，自得乾坤造化心。
廊庙乏材应见取，世无良匠勿相侵。

- 46 -

MOUNTAIN CHERRY TREE

The mountain cherry, clinging to stones,
shines through the limbs of the pines.
Among all the flowering trees
it is the last to bloom.

It hesitates, waits for a spring breeze,
refusing to flower alone,
then over the river fragrance is blown
to make its blooming known.

山樱

山樱抱石荫松枝，比并余花发最迟。
赖有春风嫌寂寞，吹香渡水报人知。

- 47 -

AMONG THE PINES
(Written while about to leave on being summoned to office)

Because I happen to search among the pines
for old poetic lines,
the witless shouldn't sing of me
the 'North Mountain Dispatch.'*

There is meaning to the emergence
of a great hero –
something that the pure recluse
could never know.

* During the Southern Qi period (479-501) a man named Zhou Yong secluded himself on North Mountain, just as Wang Anshi had stayed for a time on Mount Zhong. Later, in response to an imperial summons, Zhou came out of seclusion to become Salt Commissioner. His term of office completed; he made for the capital. When he passed by his former mountain residence a contemporary, Kong Zhigui, composed the "North Mountain Dispatch," satirizing Zhou for pretending to be a recluse when in fact he was looking forward to a handsome official salary.

Kong's piece contained the lines: "Bed curtains now empty, the cranes complain at night; The hermit now gone, the apes are startled at dawn."

松间

偶向松间觅旧题，野人休诵北山移。
丈夫出处非无意，猿鹤从来不自知。

- 48 -

PARASOL TREE IN THE AUTUMN SUN

Parasol tree in the autumn sun,
its shadow is spun like a speeding hub.

The garden, once so dark in its shade,
at next glance is bared to the light.

Cicadas chirr no more in its heights,
and on its branches jackdaws roost.

Circling it, a withered old man is seen,
singing, waiting for spring to green.

秋日在梧桐

秋日在梧桐，转阴如急毂。
冥冥蔽中庭，下视今可暴。
高蝉不复嘒，稍得寒鸦宿。
百绕有衰翁，行歌待春绿。

- 49 -

FEELINGS ON NORTH MOUNTAIN

Attachment to this mountain seems
to be my destiny,
by sovereign grace I'm now retired
back to the human world.

On the hilltop road I hesitate,
feeling deep pain,
but then, tomorrow the breeze of spring
may make its rounds again.

北山有怀

香火因缘寄北山，主恩投老更人间。
伤心踯躅冈头路，明日春风自往还。

WANG ANSHI: SELECTED POEMS

SELF-PITY 50-63

V. After Setbacks, Self-Pity.

Following setbacks in his reform agenda, self-pity arises after Wang Anshi's failure to achieve his noble humane, benevolent goals, and this leads him to the conclusion that a person's ideal state may be one of non-ambition and non-assertion, which may be the only failsafe protection against disappointment and frustration.

One of the earliest widely accepted definitions of poetry (shī) in China states that "poetry verbalizes feelings" (shī yán zhì). The very definition recognizes the cathartic function, the sense of satisfaction, or at least consolation, upon verbalizing inner feelings. The most common are: homesickness, alienation, rejection or scorn by others, as well as physical deterioration with age.

Wang's benevolent concern for widespread suffering led to his attempt to rectify injustice through ambitious systemic reforms, which generated anti-reformist resistance from conservatives as expected. Perhaps because he had fully anticipated the resistance that emerged, he was prepared to press on with the reform agenda backed by the firm support of his Emperor, although he did dutifully

王安石：诗选

自怜 50—63

V. 受挫折后，自怜

新法失败以后，王安石的崇高的、有仁心的人生目的未达到，因之产生自怜。这使他总结出：大自然的理想情况是没有雄心和不勉强。这是唯一可以保证不会失望和灰心的。

在中国，诗的一个最早的定义就是“诗言志”。这一定义承认诗有释放出内心感情的发泄作用、满意感，至少是安慰感。最普通的内心感情有：想家、疏远感、受拒或受蔑视，还有年龄大时身体的衰退等。

见到广大群众受到的苦难，王安石的仁心使他采用新法以矫正现实。其结果是受到保守派的抗拒。也许他已预见到自己的新政策会受到反抗，在明智的皇

offer to resign on more than one occasion when opposition was strongly voiced by some of the most highly respected statesmen in the empire. Still, the criticism hurt him deeply, as he was convinced of the righteousness of his cause and the appropriateness of his "New Laws." When it became clear that, for many reasons, including intentional undermining by opponents, the reform measures were not working, Wang's disappointment and pain were embodied and released in his writings, as revealed in this section's poems.

帝的支持下他努力推行这些新法。当遭到一些最有名的政治家的极力反对时，他也曾不止一次要求辞去职务。这些反抗使他大为伤心，因为他确认自己的出发点和最终目标是富有正义的，他的新法是适当的。当事实明显地表露出，因为各种原因包括他的反对者有意拆台，他的新法不能如计划进行时，王安石则将自己的失望和痛苦发泄并体现在诗词里，如这一组诗。

- 50 -

THE YELLOW CHRYSANTHEMUM STANDS SUPREME

The ball of sun above the city wall
loses light with the coming of fall.

A mass of dank air douses the sky
and plants and trees grow thin.

The yellow chrysanthemum stands supreme,
its lone blossoms defying the powers that be.

Amid the frost and dew, still shining away,
it soothes my hunger early in the day.

黄菊有至性

团团城上日，秋至少光辉。
积阴欲滔天，况乃草木微。
黄菊有至性，孤芳犯群威。
采采霜露间，亦足慰朝饥。

- 51 -

THOUGHTS ON A COOL SUMMER NIGHT ABOARD A BOAT

Dreading the heat of the day in a boat,
I lean on the mast, longing for the night.

As the sun and burning clouds withdraw
breeze and river mist turn cool.

Weary bones find relief before the coming of fall,
and a sad heart is bathed in the light of dawn.

I now have the will to face the waters ahead,
and this overflowing joy I will never forget.

夏夜舟中颇凉因有所感

扁舟畏朝热，望夜倚桅樯。
日共火云退，风兼水气凉。
未秋轻病骨，微曙浣愁肠。
坚我江湖意，滔滔兴不忘。

- 52 -

THE AUTUMN BRANCH IS LIKE A WASTED MAN

The autumn branch is like a wasted man:
complexion first reveals the haggard look,
the little chill, the blow, then nothing left,
how fragile life can be!

Better just to recollect the past
when leaves and blossoms shared their charm.
Who started this march of seasons, I wonder?
Such craving for the kill could not be Heaven's will.

秋枝如残人

秋枝如残人，颜色先憔悴。
微寒吹已空，性命一何脆。
宁当记畴昔，葩叶相妩媚。
岁行谁使然，好杀岂天意。

- 53 -

STRUGGLING TO GET UP

On a sleepless night in a cold room,
the sound of a carriage rumbles by.
I wonder who it could be
out treading the frost before me?

I heave a sigh in the pitch dark,
call for a lamp to be put by the post,
push on the pillow, struggling to get up,
and someone tells me the stars are still bright.

The sage should be hard at work with dawn's first light,
in the "Ballads of Qi" * he's up at cock's crow,
and I, alas, to scrounge for my meals,
must turn my back on a life of ideals.

* The "Ballads of Qi" refers to a section of the *Book of Songs* (Shī Jīng), the oldest anthology of Chinese poetry.

强起

寒堂耿不寐，辘辘闻车声。
不知谁家儿，先我霜上行。
叹息夜未央，遽呼置前楹。
推枕欲强起，问知星正明。
昧旦圣所勉，齐诗有鸡鸣。
嗟予以窃食，更觉负平生。

- 54 -

MOORING AT GUSU

East through Pan Gate I roam in the morning,
west through Chang Gate I leave at dusk,
no one around, for an empty stretch
I see nothing but the setting sun.

Withered trees cloaked in evening mist,
above, the call of home-bound birds.

Everything else has a place to rest –
I alone am without a nest.

泊舟姑苏

朝游盘门东，暮出阊门西。
四顾茫无人，但见白日低。
荒林带昏烟，上有归鸟啼。
物皆得所托，而我无安栖。

- 55 -

WEST ARBOR AT YIN COUNTY

No road that leads to success,
no farm to retire to,
I've spent two years
stealing food from a needy town.

I should try to be more like
sons and daughters everywhere,
enjoying the breeze and mist,
planting flowers and bamboo here and there.

鄞县西亭

收功无路去无田，窃食穷城度两年。
更作世间儿女态，乱栽花竹养风烟。

- 56 -

THE TREE WEST OF THE WALL

The tree west of the wall
throws a heavy shadow,
and my steps often bring me here
throughout the year for rest.

The sun keeps moving on,
forcing age upon me,
as the crisp winds of autumn come
and people start to fret.

Roosting birds are startled,
flutter, then reconvene,
indistinctly, the cold cicada
sobs, about to cease.

I look back at the old woods,
it has a hold on me –
how many more springs and falls
will I be here to see?

墙西树

墙西高树结阴稠，步屣穷年向此留。
白日屡移催我老，清风一至使人愁。
纷纷暝鸟惊还合，渺渺凉蝉咽欲休。
回首旧林归未得，相看知复几春秋。

- 57 -

FEELING LAZY

Feeling lazy, I close my cottage door
in late spring
as green leaves, full of shade,
suddenly fill the town.

Maybe it's just old age,
this laziness in me,
for every scene in the spring breeze
is worth the walk to see.

翛然

翛然三月闭柴荆，绿叶阴阴忽满城。
自是老年游兴少，春风何处不堪行。

- 58 -

AGAIN

I come again with my white hair
to the shady side of the wall,
even vague, scattered traces of old
are no more to be found.

Blossoms and birds always feel
the splendor of spring,
to mankind alone it remains
to feel the pain.

重将

重将白发旁墙阴，陈迹茫然不可寻。
花鸟总知春烂熳，人间独自有伤心。

- 59 -

THE BIAN RIVER FLOWS

The Bian River has no heart,
flowing away, night and day,
won't slow down to wait for me
even for a while.

I met an old friend on the way
but last night had to leave,
and who knows what land
he's entering today?

Faces are all unfamiliar
in strange lands
but cicada cries sadden
travelers everywhere.

Too bad, with all this traveling,
my goals unachieved to this day.
I set out in the world at twenty,
and now my hair is already grey.

汴水

汴水无情日夜流，不肯为我少淹留。
相逢故人昨夜去，不知今日到何州。
州州人物不相似，处处蝉鸣令客愁。
可怜南北意不就，二十起家今白头。

\- 60 -

WRITTEN AT THE FEAST OF COLD FOOD, 1052

My tangled feelings on the road
like weeping willow strands,
thousands of loose ends
in the breeze of spring.

So, at this year's Cold Food Feast
I shed tears,
enough, almost, to cause a flood
in old Nanjing.

Snow-white hair forces its way
out of my cap,
the face in my mirror, once ruddy,
is all withered now.

I've never found pleasure
in official caps and gowns,
to grow old gracefully was my only wish,
chopping firewood, catching fish.

壬辰寒食

客思似杨柳，春风千万条。
更倾寒食泪，欲涨冶城潮。
巾发雪争出，镜颜朱早凋。
未知轩冕乐，但欲老渔樵。

- 61 -

WEST WIND

When I was young, knowing nothing of fall,
I was glad to hear the west wind blow.

Old now, loaded down with troubles,
I'm frightened whenever I hear the crickets cry,
especially since I've lost my friends and loved ones,
clinging only to infirmity, traveling alone.

Midnight, and I cannot sleep,
feeling down and sorry for myself
I look up to the dark sky –
frail clouds strewn in all directions.

Soon the sleet and snow will fall
and there'll be no more stars in sight.

The seasons change so suddenly
the strongest heart is stunned,
and with no one to share their sorrows with mine,
why even bother to pour the wine?

西风

少年不知秋，喜闻西风生。
老大多感伤，畏此蟋蟀鸣。
况乃舍亲友，抱病独远行。
中夜卧不周，恻恻感我情。
起视天正黑，弱云乱纵横。
似有霰雪飘，不复星斗明。
时节忽如此，重令壮心惊。
谅无同忧人，樽酒安可倾。

- 62 -

WINTER OF 1055
WIFE AND SON BOTH SICK
STILL UNWELL AT SPRING

Heaven spins without end,
racing suns and moons,
but how many times can you turn your head
before it turns grey?

My wife and son have moaned and groaned
all through winter and spring,
I try to force a smile and a song
but don't know where to begin.

They pursue mysteries in Buddhist books,
an inexpensive vice,
rest securely in a bramble bed,
it's humble, but it's here.

Poor things, so well behaved
it's really rather sad
that all they have to show for life
is only 'not so bad.'

乙未冬妇子病至春不已

天旋无穷走日月，青发能禁几回首。
儿呻妇叹冬复春，强欲笑歌难发口。
黄卷幽寻非贵嗜，藜床稳卧虽贫有。
二物长乖亦可怜，一生所得犹多苟。

- 63 -

WHEN I WAS YOUNG

When I was young, everything was spring
all creation had a lovely air.
Though I drank no wine myself
I rejoiced with guests as they got high.

But since my temples have turned grey
hardly a joyous sight is seen,
for my heart is not the heart that was
and how the suns and moons fly by.

The very sound of merriment wears me out
and after a meal, I need to sleep.

To me, spring's return is unreal as a dream,
but no more grieving over my distress,
I offer these words to you who are young:

Be diligent in the affairs of spring,
but don't scorn a feeble elder please,
for the feeble and the strong are in two different leagues.

少年见青春

少年见青春，万物皆妩媚。
身虽不饮酒，乐与宾客醉。
一从鬓上白，百不见可喜。
心肠非故时，更觉日月驶。
闻欢已倦往，得饱还思睡。
春归只如梦，不复悲憔悴。
寄言少年子，努力作春事。
亦勿怪衰翁，衰强自然异。

NON-AMBITION AND NON-ASSERTION 64-115

VI. Mystical Awareness and Appreciation of Nature, of Non-Ambition and Non-Assertion as Nature's Ideal State.

Achieved through withdrawal from human endeavors, through observation and contemplation of natural phenomena, and through reading philosophical writings. Over time, experience, observation and reflection lead to an awareness that Nature is not only a source of healing, it is also the only valid source of truth.

For Chinese traditionally, setbacks in social or professional life lead naturally to withdrawal from urban society and a return to the less stressful rural milieu for nursing of wounds, observation and contemplation of Nature's truths, which lead to a reframing of perspective, grounded in Nature's realities, the ultimate source of "Truth" in traditional China. The Chinese word for Nature (zìrán) means literally "self-thus," which is to say "that which is what it is without intervention of will or assertion." Regarded as a pattern for human emulation, Nature becomes a model for the Taoist principle of "effortlessness" (wú wéi), or effortless achievement, most often embodied in images of flowing water and drifting clouds.

王安石：诗选

无雄心与不勉强 64—115

VI. 玄妙的觉悟和欣赏大自然，领悟到无雄心和不勉强才是大自然的理想状况

这样的觉悟和领悟是通过退出人事、观察和考虑自然现象并阅读哲学作品而达到的。经过一段时间，经验、观察和反思就会使人觉悟到大自然不但能治愈痛苦，而且也是真理的渊源。

中国古时，人在社会或职业上受到挫折就会自然脱离社会，返璞归真，以养伤和观察并思考大自然的真理。因之就会达到新的观点，并一切以大自然为本。“自然”有不受意志干预和勉强的意思。所以自然是人类学习的榜样，也是道家“无为”的原则或不费吹灰之力就能有的成绩。流水和浮云经常是“自然”的具体表现。

Taoism is the second of the "Three Teachings" (sānjiào) – Confucianism, Taoism and Buddhism (rǔ dào shì). The "Three Teachings" may be simultaneously embraced, affirmed and followed by anyone because each of them addresses different aspects of everyone's life: Confucianism aims to minimize conflict by advocating norms for social interaction as espoused by Confucius and the ancient sages; Taoism aims to minimize conflict by following the norms of Nature as espoused by Lao Zi and Zhuang Zi; and Buddhism aims to minimize everyone's suffering through enlightenment as taught by Gautama Buddha. None of the three teachings requires worship, as all three "founders" made no claim to the status of deity.

The following 52 poems are representative of Wang's mystical awareness and appreciation of Nature as a Taoist's source of truth, and a Buddhist's source of enlightenment.

道教是儒道释三教之一。任何人都可以同时信仰和追随三教，因为每一教都针对着人生中不同的一面。儒家依据孔子和先圣的教导，以社会规则减少冲突；道教依据老子和庄子的思想，以遵守大自然的规则而减少冲突；佛教则依据释迦牟尼的“通过悟真”以减少痛苦。这三教都不要求崇拜，因为其创始人都未曾自称神仙。

以下 52 首王安石的诗就代表他玄妙的觉悟和对大自然的欣赏：自然为道教真理的渊源和佛教悟真的渊源。

- 64 -

TWO MISCELLANEOUS POEMS
(Second of two poems)

Clouds appear free of care
and carefree drift away.

But the carefree mind is not to be found –
to be carefree, stop looking around.

即事二首（其二）

云从无心来，还向无心去。
无心无处寻，莫觅无心处。

- 65 -

IN A LITTLE BOAT I LET MY HAIR DOWN

In a little boat I let my hair down,
get up several times through the long night.

The Milky Way pours into the autumn-clear river,
down to the very lotus roots.

How I love glistening dewdrops
and cherish gorgeous clouds.

There's no one to join in my song, it's true,
but solitude has its pleasures too.

散发一扁舟

散发一扁舟，夜长眠屡起。
秋水泻明河，迢迢藕花底。
爱此露的皪，复怜云绮靡。
谅无与歌弦，幽独亦可喜。

- 66 -

ON BOARD A BOAT, LATE AT NIGHT

The torch draws near the other bank,
its dwindling flame illuminates the traveler's boat.

Waters bright, the fish go for bait,
sands warm, egrets forget to sleep.

A million problems crowd my mind
as I'm finally home with the dawn.

Mountain stream, if you will,
send your gentle sounds to my pillow.

舟夜即事

火炬临遥岸，余光照客船。
水明鱼中饵，沙暖鹭忘眠。
感慨无穷事，迟回欲晓天。
山泉如有意，枕上送潺湲。

- 67 -

INSCRIPTION ON A WALL IN QI'AN

Pure sunlight paints the hills,
and a warm breeze sweetens the grass.

Plum blossoms fall as flakes of snow,
wheat stalks billow as a stream of clouds.

题齐安壁

日净山如染，风暄草欲薰。
梅残数点雪，麦涨一溪云。

- 68 -

WILLOWS

Willow trees and apricot blossoms,
where are the finest found?
Near a thatch home by a stone bridge
when the rains begin to dry.

Green hangs low on a peaceful road,
rest in the deep shade there;
red blossoms inscribed on a clear pond
must be watched with care.

杨柳

杨柳杏花何处好，石梁茅屋雨初干。
绿垂静路要深驻，红写清陂得细看。

- 69 -

PLUM TREE ABOUT TO BLOOM BY THE WATERWAY

Gracefully basking in the sun
by the waterway,
lovingly restrained beauty
shines on the snow.

There's no mate, but no regrets
late into the night:
see the shadows intertwine
in the bright moonlight.

沟上梅花欲发

亭亭背暖临沟处，脉脉含芳映雪时。
莫恨夜来无伴侣，月明还见影参差。

- 70 -

IMPRESSIONS OF EARLY SUMMER

By the stone bridge a thatch hut
on a winding shore,
flowing waters gurgling
through slopes on either side.

Warm breeze and bright sun
raise an aura over the wheat,
deep green shades the dark grass –
beauty not even blossoms could surpass.

初夏即事

石梁茅屋有弯碕，流水溅溅度两陂。
晴日暖风生麦气，绿阴幽草胜花时。

- 71 -

SOUTH LAKE

By the eastern shore of South Lake
waters slowly rise,
on the road, horse and cart
no longer pass by.

Before Mount Zhong clears up
the clouds of dawn disperse;
what's to be done
in the drizzling season of the Yellow Plum.

南荡

南荡东陂水渐多，陌头车马断经过。
钟山未放朝云散，奈此黄梅细雨何。

- 72 -

NAP AT NOON

The sun above the eaves spins the shade
as a breeze blows gently at my bed.

Vague remnants of a noonday dream
and then, from somewhere, an oriole.

午睡

檐日阴阴转，床风细细吹。
倏然残午梦，何许一黄鹂。

- 73 -

TREE TIPS

Mist hangs gently on the tips of trees
on North Mountain,
water flows smoothly by grass roots
along South Brook.

Snow white strands unreeled,
mulberry trees regain a green hue,
yellow billows harvested,
paddies are now green too.

木末

木末北山烟冉冉，草根南涧水泠泠。
缫成白雪桑重绿，割尽黄云稻正青。

- 74 -

NORTH MOUNTAIN

Emerald green overflows banks
around North Mountain,
straight canal and winding pond
ripples glistening.

I sit for the longest while,
watching blossoms fall,
then leisurely look for herbs to pick
and don't come home until late.

北山

北山输绿涨横陂，直堑回塘滟滟时。
细数落花因坐久，缓寻芳草得归迟。

- 75 -

SOUTH COVE
(First of two poems)

South Cove, East Knoll,
second month of spring,
the splendid view draws a few
lines of poetry.

Emerald green embraces the breeze,
ripples clear and clean,
tender twigs toy with sunlight,
dangling long and lean.

南浦（其一）

南浦东风二月时，物华撩我有新诗。
含风鸭绿鳞鳞起，弄日鹅黄袅袅垂。

- 76 -

SOUTH COVE
(Second of two poems)

Following the blossoms into South Cove
my boat goes astray and I lose my way.

Mysterious fragrance from someplace unknown,
and west of the painted bridge – sundown.

南浦（其二）

南浦随花去，回舟路已迷。
暗香无觅处，日落画桥西。

- 77 -

A SKETCH

The path was warm, with woven weeds around,
the mountain clear, with blossoms everywhere.

A stream meandered by at will
and up and down the hillside were several village homes.

As I rested in the stillness, a cock crowed at noon,
deeper in the bush, a dog barked at dusk.

When I came home I told folks
I felt I had been to Utopia*.

* Utopia: The reference is to the celebrated Peach Blossom Village, an agrarian Utopia of Chinese legend.

即事

径暖草如积，山晴花更繁。
纵横一川水，高下数家村。
静憩鸡鸣午，荒寻犬吠昏。
归来向人说，疑是武陵源。

- 78 -

RESIDING BY THE DINGLIN MONASTERY

A winding brook surrounds the house,
bamboo enfolds the mountain,
brook and mountain both are up
high among the clouds.

I head for the brook, bring out the boat
and glide by the mountainside,
brookside birds, mountainside blossoms
all as idle as I.

定林所居

屋绕湾溪竹绕山，溪山却在白云间。
临溪放艇依山坐，溪鸟山花共我闲。

- 79 -

EVENING STROLL BY MOUNT ZHONG

Drizzle and breeze
fell chinaberry blossoms,
like delicate red snowflakes,
speckling the sandy shore.

Hibiscus fence, bamboo hut,
river village road,
now and then a tavern
selling local wine.

钟山晚步

小雨轻风落楝花，细红如雪点平沙。
槿篱竹屋江村路，时见宜城卖酒家。

- 80 -

ENJOYING MOUNT ZHONG

I watch the mountain all day long,
never tire of it.
I bought the mountain as a place
to while away old age.

Mountain blossoms all fall,
the mountain stands tall;
mountain streams flow at will,
the mountain stands still.

游钟山

终日看山不厌山，买山终待老山间。
山花落尽山长在，山水空流山自闲。

- 81 -

RETURNING ALONE

I come home alone to Mount Zhong
in a dim mist,
rice paddies crowd the hills,
half brown, half green.

A tired farmer knows deep down
the water's not enough,
but he keeps on pedaling the pump,
watching clouds go by.

How sad! He labors
so hard and long all year,
the evening song, like wailing,
is painful to hear.

But I am free from office,
blessed with idleness
by the north window on a pillowed mat
where the breeze is fresh and clean.

Now and then, lotus blossoms
squeeze through stems and leaves,
little ripples tease the snowy froth,
countless forms of beauty.

Who can come and doze with me,
share in this pleasure?
Waters are shallow in autumn, yes,
but they still can hold a boat.

独归

钟山独归雨微冥，稻畦夹冈半黄青。
疲农心知水未足，看云倚木车不停。
悲哉作劳亦已久，暮歌如哭难为听。
而我官闲幸无事，北窗枕簟风泠泠。
於时荷花拥翠盖，细浪翾雪千娉婷。
谁能欹眠共此乐，秋港虽浅可扬舲。

\- 82 -

RESTING ALONE
(First of two poems)

What's the use of hoe and harrow
if you only let them lie?
My pitiful garden's
given over to weeds.

I'd like to find a view of spring
but the paths are overgrown,
so I face the climbing sun
resting on a couch, alone.

独卧（二首之一）

谁有锄耰不自操，可怜园地满蓬蒿。
欲寻春物无蹊径，独卧南床白日高。

- 83 -

OUT TO THE COUNTRYSIDE

The whole stretch of prairie land
is laced with green,
trees grow thick and full,
no blossoms to be seen.

Sunlight and breeze, filled with feeling,
looking for something to touch,
they first bestow themselves upon
mulberry and hemp.

出郊

川原一片绿交加，深树冥冥不见花。
风日有情无处著，初回光景到桑麻。

- 84 -

BY A STREAM ON MOUNT TIANTONG

Stream water rippling pure,
trees all green,
I stroll through the river woods,
tread the spring scene.

The stream grows deep, the woods thick
in a place with no one near,
only the scent of distant blossoms
crosses the water here.

天童山溪上

溪水清涟树老苍，行穿溪树踏春阳。
溪深树密无人处，唯有幽花渡水香。

- 85 -

IN THE MOUNTAINS

I follow the moon up into the mountains,
search for clouds to join me going home.

A spring morning, dew on flower petals –
the fragrance clings to my gown.

山中

随月出山去，寻云相伴归。
春晨花上露，芳气著人衣。

\- 86 -

A SKETCH OF MOUNT ZHONG

Silently, the mountain stream
circles the bamboo grove,
west of the bamboo, flowers and grasses
play around with spring.

I sit under thatched eaves
facing this all day,
without a single bird's call
the mountain's mystery grows.

钟山即事

涧水无声绕竹流，竹西花草弄春柔。
茅檐相对坐终日，一鸟不鸣山更幽。

- 87 -

NIGHT WATCH

Incense burnt in the golden urn,
water-clock run dry,
a light breeze swishes time and again
cool upon cool.

The lustre of spring provokes me,
keeps me awake,
and the moon moves flower shadows
up the banister.

夜直

金炉香尽漏声残，翦翦轻风阵阵寒。
春色恼人眠不得，月移花影上栏干。

- 88 -

RESTING ALONE
(Second of two poems)

Noonday shadow of thatched eaves
slowly shifts around,
moss grows at my gate,
a stream runs by at will.

An oriole warbles on and on,
can't be seen at all,
countless crabapple blossoms
emerge over the wall.

独卧（二首之二）

茅檐午影转悠悠，门闭青苔水乱流。
百啭黄鹂看不见，海棠无数出墙头。

- 89 -

FROM THE DINGLIN TEMPLE, PASSING BY THE WEST CONVENT

No mid-day cock's crow
is heard in the Buddhist temple,
sleeping in stillness
amid the vapor of cedar incense.

Suddenly I recall the words
of the Westcliff Priest:
Staff in hand, when the spirit moves you,
there are mysteries to pursue.

自定林过西庵

午鸡声不到禅林，柏子烟中静拥衾。
忽忆西岩道人语，杖藜乘兴得幽寻。

- 90 -

LYRICS FOR THE TUNE "HUAN XI SHA"

The courtyard, a hundred acres
half under moss,
out in front a pale stream
lingers leisurely.
How few love idleness enough
to come this way!

A winding hall around a small courtyard
in a lonely silent spring,
mountain peach and riverside almond,
two or three in all,
for whom do they blossom,
for whom do they fall?

浣溪沙

百亩中庭半是苔，门前白道水萦回，爱闲能有几人来。
小院回廊春寂寂，山桃溪杏两三栽，为谁零落为谁开。

- 91 -

AT LEISURE

It's good to breakfast late when you have the time,
late in life, one needn't rise with the sun.

Others may tease me that my belly sags,
but I'm just glad I can still bend my arms.

Though I can't get rid of the Snake of Sleep,
I'm never bothered by the Viper of Dreams.

Tell the dwellers in the woods what I say:
Think Zen, and you'll keep sickness away.

身闲

身闲宜晚食，岁晏忌晨兴。
人自嘲便腹，吾方乐曲肱。
睡蛇虽不去，梦虺已无凭。
寄语中林客，思禅病未能。

- 92 -

GARDEN OF ENLIGHTENMENT

Swollen, swirling waters
rinse the porch,
a dream by the window fades
to bird calls at noon.

Day after day, fragrant grasses
are inspired by the breeze of spring,
and north and south of the hill
paths are vanishing.

悟真院

野水纵横漱屋除，午窗残梦鸟相呼。
春风日日吹香草，山北山南路欲无。

- 93 -

TWO MISCELLANEOUS POEMS
(First of two poems)

Clouds are born upon Mount Zhong
but also return to this high ground.

Tell me, hermit of the hills,
where can the clouds be found?

即事二首（其一）

云从钟山起，却入钟山去。
借问山中人，云今在何处。

- 94 -

TWENTY POEMS IN THE STYLE OF HAN SHAN AND SHI DE (Second of 20 poems)

If I were an ox or a horse
I'd rejoice over grass and beans.

If, on the other hand, I were a woman,
the sight of men would please me.

As long as I am true to myself
I'll always settle for being me.

If taste and distaste keep you upset,
surely you are being used:

Gentlemen, with your heads in the stars,
don't confuse what you have with what you are!

拟寒山拾得二十首（其二）

我曾为牛马，见草豆欢喜。
又曾为女人，欢喜见男子。
我若真是我，只合长如此。
若好恶不定，应知为物使。
堂堂大丈夫，莫认物为己。

- 95 -

TWENTY POEMS IN THE STYLE OF HAN SHAN AND SHI DE (Sixteenth of 20 poems)

Beat a thief, and he'll be scared to death,
entertain a guest, and he'll be overjoyed,
but guests can be thieves, you know,
never be fooled by their deceits!

How lucky, then, to be born poor,
duty-free, unburdened heart and soul,
never a thief you have to beat,
never a guest you have to cajole.

拟寒山拾得二十首（其十六）

打贼贼恐怖，看客客喜欢。
亦有客是贼，切莫受伊谩。
乐哉贫儿家，无事役心肝。
既无贼可打，岂有客须看。

- 96 -

LIFE

Life gets so complicated
as we grow old,
short on talent, what advice
could I possibly offer you?

Riding a horse along South Road
where the yellow dust enshrouds,
nothing appeals to the eye except
North Mountain clouds.

人间

人间投老事纷纷，才薄何能强致君。
一马黄尘南陌路，眼中唯见北山云。

- 97 -

THE AUTUMN SUN IS OUT OF SIGHT

The autumn sun is out of sight,
just a trace of yellow left above the woods.

I lean on a staff, longing for the plains,
looking up and down, afraid of losing light.

A breeze zips over the valley brook,
puffs at my robe and gown.

Gracefully lighting up the frost on my cap,
the mountain moon shines down.

秋日不可见

秋日不可见，林端但余黄。
杖藜思平野，俯仰畏无光。
栗栗涧谷风，吹我衣与裳。
娟娟空山月，照我冠上霜。

- 98 -

TWENTY POEMS IN THE STYLE OF HAN SHAN AND SHI DE (Eleventh of 20 poems)

Puppets are gadgets and nothing more,
none of their kind has roots to tend,
for I have been behind their stage
and seen with my own eyes.

Then I discovered the audience,
all their excitement completely controlled,
fooled by puppets through the whole play,
tricked into tossing their wealth away.

拟寒山拾得二十首（其十一）

傀儡只一机，种种没根栽。
被我入棚中，昨日亲看来。
方知棚外人，扰扰一场呆。
终日受伊谩，更被索钱财。

- 99 -

WRITTEN IN REPLY TO CHEN ZHENGSHU USING HIS OWN RHYMES
(First of two poems)

My black robe has a haggard look
as I make my way back north,
hair frosted to the roots,
face covered with dust.

I came to hate mad dogs
after the whole pack howled,
and none recognized the call
of a Dragon Steed.

Fame and merit are so remote
they lie beyond pursuit
as suns and moons drift on and on
never to return.

The chance for greatness came,
and so near to me,
I open my wine and poetry
both frequently.

次韵答陈正叔（二首之一）

青衫憔悴北归来，发有霜根面有埃。
群吠我方憎猘子，一鸣谁更识龙媒。
功名落落求难值，日月沄沄去不回。
胜事与身何等近，酒樽诗卷数须开。

- 100 -

WHILING AWAY THE TIME

I close the door to shut out sorrow
but sorrow won't go away.

Strange, but when the spring breeze comes,
try to retain it, and sorrow won't stay.

自遣

闭户欲推愁，愁终不肯去。
底事春风来，留愁愁不住。

- 101 -

INSCRIPTION ON THE WALL OF HALFWAY MOUNTAIN TEMPLE (First of two poems)

Every time I go out, it rains,
and when I don't, it shines.

It couldn't be the rain falls for me,
no, we just happen on each other every time.

题半山寺壁（二首之一）

我行天即雨，我止雨还住。
雨岂为我行，邂逅与相遇。

- 102 -

INSCRIPTION ON THE WALL OF HALFWAY MOUNTAIN TEMPLE (Second of two poems)

Cold, we seek to sit in the warmth,
hot, we head for the cool:

everything that lives is Buddha
and Buddha is all that lives.

题半山寺壁（二首之二）

寒时暖处坐，热时凉处行。
众生不异佛，佛即是众生。

- 103 -

TWENTY POEMS IN THE STYLE OF HAN SHAN AND SHI DE (Fourth of 20 poems)

The wind blew, and a tile fell off the roof,
gave me a gash right on top of my head,
but the tile smashed itself to bits as well,
so mine was not the only blood to spill,
and I do not curse it after all,
since the tile didn't intentionally fall.

All such hating is our own creation,
often drawn from a single fluke,
but accidents happen and we, unaware,
feel that blame must be placed somewhere,
and this always leads to a tragic end,
I ask you, please, cultivate this truth,
and never again will you lose your way,
and never will hatred lead you astray.

拟寒山拾得二十首（其四）

风吹瓦堕屋，正打破我头。
瓦亦自破碎，岂但我血流。
我终不嗔渠，此瓦不自由。
众生造众恶，亦有一机抽。
渠不知此机，故自认愆尤。
此但可哀怜，劝令真正修。
岂可自迷闷，与渠作冤仇。

- 104 -

REVERSIBLE VERSE
(Readable left to right from top to bottom, and right to left from bottom to top)

moon pops out…
riverfish scared
leap up
clouds split
and startle
hills full
of birds

paths steep
in weeds
growing wild
steps ruined
among charming
blossoms teeming

迸月（回文诗）

迸月川鱼跃，开云岭鸟翻。
径斜荒草恶，台废冶花繁。

- 105 -

EAST RIDGE

I climb East Ridge at year's end
to enjoy the long view
and gaze upon an endless river
shining through distant woods:

angry howls from a million mouths
– winds blow my lament,
thousands of waves surge again and again,
though the stream has no intent.

东冈

东冈岁晚一登临，共望长河映远林。
万窍怒号风丧我，千波竞涌水无心。

- 106 -

ON A SPRING DAY

Waters rise in spring
north and south of the pond,
time to go for slow strolls
through groves of blossoming peach.

So much petty fretting
over matters dreamt up in the mind,
why worry over nothing but a name
that will just be left behind?

春日即事

池北池南春水生，桃花深处好闲行。
细思扰扰梦中事，何用悠悠身后名。

- 107 -

GHOST TOWN

Looking back at the ghost town,
how far away,
I remember it as a nice place
I used to pass through.

I really miss East Mountain,
the texture of trees in mist,
I miss South Lake even more
with its autumn-clear ripples.

A hundred years have brought it down
like a shattered dream that was.
But all things eventually go astray,
so why sing sad songs?

Better just to drink the wine,
mention it no more,
there's plenty of bright moonlight
over the river tonight.

孤城

孤城回望距几何，记得好处常经过。
最思东山烟树色，更忆南湖秋水波。
百年颠倒如梦寐，万事乖隔徒悲歌。
应须饮酒不复道，今夜江头明月多。

- 108 -

BOATRIDE
Written at a Banquet, Using the Rhyme Words of Weizhi's Poem

Riding in a banquet boat
we probe the depths for Northern Orchards,
ask a Buddhist monk
about ancient remains.

We disembark and follow a moat
along a twisted way,
the sky touches mountain peaks,
the view is dizzying.

In the old kingdom times were peaceful
and the woods were unused,
but few remain in the run-down city,
more like a village now.

Always and ever rise and fall
are of this kind,
let's just drown our dried-up sorrows
in a cup of wine.

即席次韵微之泛舟

画舸幽寻北果园，应将陈迹问桑门。
地随墙壁行多曲，天著冈峦望易昏。
故国时平空有木，荒城人少半为村。
悠悠兴废皆如此，赖付干愁酒一樽。

- 109 -

LYRICS FOR THE TUNE "PUSA MAN"

Several thatched homes
laze near the riverside,
thin gown and common cap
mingle with weeping willow trees.

Wonder whose house rules the land today?
I watch myself crossing the stone bridge
as a young moon tapers down slow.

Drunk all day, I sober up at dusk,
and what touches me most?
The warble of a yellow oriole.

菩萨蛮

数家茅屋闲临水。单衫短帽垂杨里。今日是何朝。看予度石桥。
梢梢新月偃。午醉醒来晚。何物最关情。黄鹂一两声。

- 110 -

LYRICS FOR THE TUNE "NAN XIANG ZI" (Second of two poems)

For ages, the land of kings,
floating in a blessed aura
of fullness and plenty,
four hundred years, and now
nothing but a dream.
So sad!

Jin Dynasty caps and gowns
now burial mounds.

I wander at will along a winding stream,
and climb to the top of a city wall
and to the top of its tower.

The past is so remote,
don't even ask where it goes,
just turn around:

beyond the railing, only the Yangtze
River still flows.

南乡子二首（其二）

自古帝王州，郁郁葱葱佳气浮。
四百年来成一梦，堪愁。晋代衣冠成古丘。
绕水恣行游。上尽层城更上楼。
往事悠悠君莫问，回头。槛外长江空自流。

- 111 -

THE GAME OF CHESS

Never let a mere game
hurt feelings that are real,
better to take things as they come
and then cry "I win!"

After a battle, when the whites and blacks
are put back in their box,
where on the board does there remain
a trace of loss or gain?

棋

莫将戏事扰真情，且可随缘道我赢。
战罢两奁分白黑，一枰何处有亏成。

- 112 -

FRESH FLOWERS

Pleasures are few enough in old age,
all the fewer when you're sick in bed.

I draw some water, arrange fresh flowers,
find consolation in their drifting fragrance.

But drifting fragrance only stays a while,
and me, how long is my lot?

Fresh flowers and old me –
Enough! Let us both be forgot.

新花

老年少忻豫，况复病在床。
汲水置新花，取慰以流芳。
流芳只须臾，我亦岂久长。
新花与故吾，已矣两可忘。

- 113 -

SHOWN TO WU YUAN ON THE TERRACE

Fine print frustrates an old reader's eyes,
and a long mattress lures him to a deep sleep.

Go for the mat and take the nap,
chuck the bookish truth and get back to youth.

台上示吴愿

细书妨老读，长簟惬昏眠。
取簟且一息，抛书还少年。

- 114 -

WRITTEN IN REPLY TO A POEM BY DENG ZIYI USING HIS OWN RHYME WORDS (First of two poems)

We were both in the spring of life
when we met at Green Brook,
aging now, as I face the stream
my spirit suddenly fails.

Things just happen and pass away
wave after wave,
years come and bring no more
than new grey hairs.

To tell the truth, I cannot bear
to turn my back on angry eyes,
but in governing I really fear
approaching bristled scales.

Thank you for the fine lines
that offer such good will,
I only regret I can be no more
than merely run of the mill.

次韵酬邓子仪二首（其一）

青溪相值各青春，老去临流辄损神。
事事只随波浪去，年年空得鬓毛新。
论心未忍遗横目，干世还忧近逆鳞。
嘉句感君邀我厚，自嗟才不异常人。

- 115 -

IN ACADEMICIAN CHEN'S LITTLE GARDEN, ECHOING HIS OWN RHYMES

No exotic bird calls
come from the eaves,
and not a single frog is heard
croaking by the pond;

trees retain the evening rain
as colors come and go,
plants lean into the morning sun
as green is born again.

Everything fits into Nature's scheme
nothing should be mourned,
hopes and fears of our hundred years
are best left ignored.

You and I, staff in hand,
watch the Change appear,
scratching our heads in the spring breeze,
our eyes, at least, still clear.

次韵陈学士小园即事

墙屋虽无好鸟鸣，池塘亦未有蛙声。
树含宿雨红初入，草倚朝阳绿更生。
万物天机何得丧，百年心事不将迎。
与君杖策聊观化，搔首春风眼尚明。

AWARENESS 116-126

VII. Awareness that Even the Distinctions between Illusion and Reality are False.

This level of awareness requires a loftier vision than the mere recognition that Nature's non-assertive Way (the Way of Water) is most enlightened. Chinese thinkers, particularly Taoists and Buddhists, have for centuries been concerned with the folly of our efforts to make clear and valid distinctions between illusion and reality, and by extension, falsehood and truth. The first lines of Lao Zi's Taoist classic state unequivocally that "truths may be told, but never lasting Truth; words may be uttered, but never lasting words." In other words, reality (Truth) is not something that can be defined in words because it is not a thing, but a process that is always in flux. Most of the parables in *Zhuang Zi* illustrate an aspect of this principle, the most famous being the "Butterfly Dream," wherein there is a titillating uncertainty whether the speaker is Zhuang Zi who has just awakened from a dream in which he was a butterfly, or is indeed a real butterfly now dreaming he is Zhuang Zi. Is our "reality" something we wake up to from illusory dreams, or is our "waking state" an illusion that is in fact now being dreamt?

王安石：诗选

觉悟 116—126

VII. 觉悟到“幻觉”和“现实”的区别其实是虚假的

这一层次的觉悟需要更高的视野，而不仅仅是认识到大自然的行云流水是最开朗的。几世纪以来中国有高见的思想家，特别是道家和佛家，都在思考着我们努力地辨别幻觉和现实是否为荒谬之举。也就是说，辨别虚假和真理是否是荒谬的。老子在《道德经》里清楚明白地说：“道可道，非常道。名可名，非常名。”换句话说，实际（真理）是不能用语言定名的，因为它不是什么具体的东西；它是随时都在变化的。《庄子》一书里的寓言主要阐明了这一点。此书里最著名的寓言就是“蝴蝶梦”。这个故事说的是不知叙述者是庄子从梦到自己是蝴蝶的梦中醒来，还是那只蝴蝶竟然

For many people this can be a dangerous and unsettling awareness, for our most fundamental beliefs, upon which nearly all our conscious decisions and actions are based, assume the validity of distinctions between right and wrong, true and false, real and imaginary, and countless other frames of reference using "either/or" dichotomies. Chinese society was for millennia managed by thinkers who donned official (Confucianist) caps for making "either/or" distinctions while on duty, and after work switched to Taoist and Buddhist modes of thought for contemplating the higher truths that lie beyond such neat distinctions. "Either/or" dichotomies are most useful for maintaining a sense of order and for getting things done, while rejection of such distinctions is also necessary to alert people that "Change" has left static categories behind, creating discrepancies between old and new realities. Wang Anshi reminds himself of the deceptive nature of surface "realities" in many of his poems.

梦着它是庄子。我们的“现实”是梦幻醒来后的现实？还是我们的“醒觉”是我们的梦幻？

对很多人来说，这是一种危险而于心不安的觉悟，因为几乎我们所有的有意识的决定和行动所依据的基本信念都认为对错、真假、实虚等“是与非”的辨别是正确的。几千年来，治理中国的思想家都是在工作时以儒家思想做着“是与非”的区别，工作后则以道家和佛家的思考方式去追求比这种辨别更高的真理。“是与非”的区别在保持秩序和要有作为时很有用；但排斥这类区别也是有必要的。原因是，可以警醒人们现实是随时在“变”的，并且，常出现新的现实是不可避免的。王安石在他的许多诗中就提醒他自己，生活中那种表面上的所谓“现实”其实是虚假的。

- 116 -

AFTER SPRING RAIN

Young spring, ten days of rain,
the weather breaks, my door is open wide,
calmly I gaze at the patterns of green moss.

Moss!
Stay down!
Grow away from my gown!

春晴

新春十日雨，雨晴门始开。
静看苍苔纹，莫上人衣来。

- 117 -

A CONVERSATION WITH GENG TIANZHI

Forty years
in a naptime dream*
you wake up and find the millet
not quite cooked.

The myriad affairs of life
are bird tracks in the air,
why on earth should you recall
and recount them all.

* Forty years in a naptime dream: The reference is to a popular tale, "Handan Dream," in which a poor scholar spent a lifetime in a dream, while in "reality" less time had passed than it took to cook a pot of yellow millet (sometimes this tale is also referred to as a "Yellow Millet Dream"), a reminder of the illusory nature of human experience.

与耿天骘会话

邯郸四十余年梦，相对黄粱欲熟时。
万事只如空鸟迹，怪君强记尚能追。

- 118 -

COMPOSED IN A DREAM

A dark cloud cover grows
north of Green Gate Road,
then I see huge cabinets
filled with jugs of wine.

The Mountain Dragon makes rainwaters rise
axle-high on the road.
Not selling the wine doesn't worry me,
I just worry that this dream will cease to be.

梦中作

青门道北云为屋，大垆贮酒千万斛。
独龙注雨如车轴，不畏不售畏不续。

- 119 -

COUNTY BRIDGE

Crossing County Bridge, stepping over the moon,
I thought of pepper trees,
looked back toward a sad murmur,
mountain shallows seemed near.

Tonight once again I hear
sobs from long ago
and seeing the moon above a mountain
talk of County Bridge.

州桥

州桥蹋月想山椒，回首哀湍未觉遥。
今夜重闻旧呜咽，却看山月话州桥。

- 120 -

ON THE RIVER

North of the River, autumn's dank shadow
clears halfway,
but evening clouds, full of rain,
still remain.

In a tangle of green mountains
the way seems to disappear,
then suddenly a thousand other sails,
now there, now here.

江上

江北秋阴一半开，晚云含雨却低回。
青山缭绕疑无路，忽见千帆隐映来。

- 121 -

SPRING BREEZE

On a lone horse heading north
in the spring breeze,
I have a feeling I'm among
familiar hills and streams.

The sun floats beyond the trees
above the wide river,
dust rises over the plain
and smoke from wilderness fires.

Tender yellow, lent by the sun,
begins to touch the willows,
new green, urged by the rain,
returns to the fields.

I turn around and look again,
find no magnolia trees,
then remember that last year
I was viewing blossoms here.

春风

一马春风北首燕，却疑身得旧山川。
阳浮树外沧江水，尘涨原头野火烟。
日借嫩黄初著柳，雨催新绿稍归田。
回头不见辛夷发，始觉看花是去年。

- 122 -

SONG OF THE ROYAL CONSORT
(Second of two poems)

The Royal Consort was wedded
to a nomad boy
with a hundred felt-covered carriages
filled with Tatar maids.

She tried to reveal the depths of her soul
but no one understood,
so she poured the feelings she alone knew
all into her lute.

Her golden pick strummed sounds
sweeter than the breeze of spring
while she watched wild geese fly away
as she poured Tatar wine.

Her Han Palace maidservants
shed silent tears
and travelers on desert sands
turned their heads her way.

Then her feelings for the Han grew weak,
for the Tatars deep
since happiness is found in life
where the heart is at home.

Now her pitiful Azure Tomb
is overgrown, wasted away,
but the mournful sound of her lute strings
rings to this very day.

明妃曲二首（其二）

明妃初嫁与胡儿，毡车百辆皆胡姬。
含情欲语独无处，传与琵琶心自知。
黄金杆拨春风手，弹看飞鸿劝胡酒。
汉宫侍女暗垂泪，沙上行人却回首。
汉恩自浅胡恩深，人生乐在相知心。
可怜青冢已芜没，尚有哀弦留至今。

- 123 -

ON THE OCCASION OF WATCHING ACTORS in the Xingxiang Courtyard of the Qixiangtianjie Hall at Xiangguo Temple

Actors standing on the stage,
this one noble, that one low:

knowing deep down they are the same,
they neither rejoice nor complain.

相国寺启向天节道场行香院观戏者

侏优戏场中，一贵复一贱。
心知本自同，所以无欣怨。

- 124 -

TWENTY POEMS IN THE STYLE OF HAN SHAN AND SHI DE (Seventh of 20 poems)

I have read a million books
seeking to learn all there is to know,
but the wise always seem to keep it to themselves,
and who would listen to the other fools?

How marvelous, the people of the Idle Way,
who leap clear of each restraining clause,
who know that Truth lies deep in themselves
and can never come from someplace else.

拟寒山拾得二十首（其七）

我读万卷书，识尽天下理。
智者渠自知，愚者谁信尔。
奇哉闲道人，跳出三句里。
独悟自根本，不从他处起。

- 125 -

TWENTY POEMS IN THE STYLE OF HAN SHAN AND SHI DE (Fifteenth of 20 poems)

It's hard to be happy when you're down and out,
and easy to go wrong once you gain sway.

After suffering pain, pleasure is what we need,
but pleasure, then, gives birth to greed.

I know neither pleasure nor pain;
I am neither enlightened nor dim.

I am neither attached to the Three Levels of Life*,
nor do I try to transcend them.

* The Three Levels of Life are: the worlds of sensuous desire, of form, and the formless world of pure spirit.

拟寒山拾得二十首（其十五）

失志难作福，得势易造罪。
苦即念快乐，乐即生贪爱。
无苦亦无乐，无明亦无昧。
不属三界中，亦非三界外。

- 126 -

CLIMBING BAOGONG PAGODA

Worn out pageboy and tired horse
left behind at the Gate of Pines,
I cling to a bamboo pole alone
and lean on a pillar of stone.

The river moon rolls through the sky
with the light of day,
clouds above the mountain peaks
divide the dark and dusk.

A mouse rattles the silence
and other sounds arise,
crows steady their wilderness perch
and shadows flutter below.

Here, where notions like guest and host
are hardly ever heard,
the priest forgets about the "I"
and I forget the word.

登宝公塔

倦童疲马放松门，自把长筇倚石根。
江月转空为白昼，岭云分暝与黄昏。
鼠摇岑寂声随起，鸦矫荒寒影对翻。
当此不知谁客主，道人忘我我忘言。

RECONCILIATION 127-130

VIII. Fully Aware of the Illusory, Enigmatic Nature of the Human Situation, Still Finding Life Attractive, and Being Willing to Live with the Enigma.

People need to have things to look forward to, so after a while contemplating the ultimate futility of human endeavor is not much fun. After work, we may meditate on the inscrutability of the universe in our spare time, but during working hours we have to try to make things work, and when the times and conditions are right, they may indeed work. This may be the most mature form of enlightenment revealed in Wang Anshi's poetry, and useful, perhaps, as the cornerstone of a mellow philosophy of life.

"Truth" with a capital T is something we seem neuro-chemically conditioned to seek and enjoy, even though ultimately we should speak only of each person's (or generation's, or civilization's) inventory of "small t" truths, each useful only in particular contexts. Still, "truth" and other such "either/or" concepts are useful, indeed indispensable, as frames of reference for achieving everyday goals in life. Therefore they should neither be discarded nor uncritically accepted.

王安石：诗选

和解 127—130

VIII. 完全觉察到人类情况的变幻和奥秘，但仍觉生命的吸引力，所以愿意与奥秘共存

人们需要有可展望的事情，只沉思人的徒劳无功是无益于事的。工作后可以思虑宇宙的神秘；工作时，却得使事情顺当。况且时间和条件都对时，事情竟然确实会顺当。这也许是王安石诗词中最成熟的觉悟，也是最有益的，也许是随遇而安的人生哲学的基石。

大真理好像是我们自然要追寻和喜爱的。然而每个人、每一世代或每一文明终究还是要创造自己的许多小真理；每一个小真理在某种情况下都各有它的用途。小真理和“是与非”这样的观念是有用的，甚至是不可或缺的，它可以作为达到生活目的的准则。所

This enlightened awareness and resulting enjoyment of the paradoxical human situation is implicit in several of Wang's poems. This is consistent with the findings of prize-winning physicists of the past century who have demonstrated that insistence on neat and rigorous "either/or" frames of analysis are of limited use in the quest for lasting truths. Still, even quantum physicists such as 1932 Nobel Prize winner Werner Heisenberg, would have trouble making day-to-day decisions without "either/or" frames of reference. Therefore, they use them reluctantly.

以不应该将之丢弃，但也不应该随便接受它。

这种受启发的觉悟和随之而来的对人生矛盾的享用（接纳）与20世纪得奖的物理学家的发现是一致的。他们已论证出：坚持绝对的是与非的对立在寻求基本真理时只有有限的用处。王安石的几首诗中也隐含着这个意思。然而，如果没有是与非的准则，就连量子物理学家，如1932年诺贝尔物理学奖得主维尔纳·海森堡，虽然不太情愿，也很难做出日常生活中的决定。所以是与非的准则还是有必要的。

- 127 -

STAFF IN HAND

Staff in hand, I follow the river
around East Ridge,
when the fun is done I come home
and head straight to bed,

but the pros and cons of kings and tyrants
still invade my dreams
and let me know that ways long set
are not forgotten yet.

杖藜

杖藜随水转东冈，兴罢还来赴一床。
尧桀是非时入梦，固知余习未全忘。

- 128 -

TWENTY POEMS IN THE STYLE OF HAN SHAN AND SHI DE (Tenth of 20 poems)

Yesterday I saw Zhang San
and resented his lack of restraint,
but when I came home I repented,
knowing such judgments are wrong.

Then today, when I saw Zhang San
the urge to judge arose again.

If this bad habit could be put down
there'd be very few Buddhists around.

拟寒山拾得二十首（其十）

昨日见张三，嫌他不守己。
归来自悔责，分别亦非理。
今日见张三，分别心复起。
若除此恶习，佛法无多子。

- 129 -

TO MASTER LI

Master Li is a wealthy man
and a poor boy too,
others don't know him
as well as I do.

He leaps over the Dharma Wheels,
plays among the cliffs,
beyond enlightenment he is cool
like a raving fool.

寄李道人

李生富汉亦贫儿，人不知渠只我知。
跳过六轮中耍峭，养成三界外愚痴。

\- 130 -

ALLEGORY
(First of two poems)

Nothing in the universe can be figured out,
leaves drop, while pine branches scoff at old age.

Still, a blossoming peach makes me feel like a sage.
Here is one without a doubt still having doubts.

寓言二首（其一）

太虚无实可追寻，叶落松枝谩古今。
若见桃花生圣解，不疑还自有疑心。

POSTSCRIPT

Dreams historically have played a very important role in Chinese folklore, legends, fiction and poetry, so of course we find frequent reference to dreams in the poems and lyrics of Wang Anshi. For example, in his poem "To a Friend" (#17), we see:

The river pushes streams of tears
flowing out to sea,
winds blow a dreaming soul
all the way home.

To fully appreciate this image, we need to understand how traditional Chinese understood the dream phenomenon, which is quite simple and rational: When we are asleep, our soul (hún) can leave our body by exiting through the fontanelle (the space between the frontal and parietal bones of the skull). What the soul encounters, sees and hears during its separation from the body are what we dream while asleep. Viewed this way, the line "winds blow a dreaming soul all the way home" makes perfect sense.

后记

梦在中国的民间故事、传说、小说和诗词里一直非常重要。我们在王安石的诗词中就注意到梦有着重要的地位。比如，在他的《寄友人》（17）一诗中就有“江拥涕洟流入海，风吹魂梦去还家”的诗句提到“魂梦”。

传统上，中国古人对梦的解释其实是相当简单而合理的。他们认为，人睡觉时，魂就从囟门（头颅前骨和颅顶骨之间的地方）出去。这样，魂游时所遇、所见和所闻的就是人的梦。所以，王安石诗中的“风吹魂梦去还家”是很有道理的。

Turning attention now to the roles or functions of dreams in Wang's poems, we find several. One of the most common is the dream as a source of satisfaction substituting for an unsatisfactory reality. On the surface, this sounds like Freud's "wish fulfillment," which is often manifested through the dream mechanism, but in Wang's poems it is different: it does not come from the unconscious but is done intentionally. For example, after thoroughly enjoying himself on a visit with friends to Lake View Pavilion in Hangzhou (#18 "Composed on Horseback"), returning home he writes:

Hereafter this can only enter
into my dreams,
for there I still can enjoy myself
with my old friends.

In another poem (#22 "Returning Home"), lamenting the requirements for a government official to be on the road and far from home so much of the time, he concludes:

How to forget this bridled roaming?
by staying carefree in drunken dreams.

王安石诗词中的“梦”有几种作用。最普遍的是梦中的满意代表现实中不满意的事情。表面上看来，这很像心理学家弗洛伊德所说的由做梦而达到“愿望的实现”。然而，在王安石的诗中却有所不同，因为这种梦不是不知不觉做的，而是有意做的。例如，他和朋友在杭州望湖楼痛痛快快游玩后，回到家写出《杭州望湖楼回马上作呈玉汝乐道》（18），诗云：“从此只应长入梦，梦中还与故人游。”在另一首诗《还家》（22）中，他写道：“何以忘羁旅，翛然醉梦间。”

Other times, the dream may function as an irritant that runs counter to the poet's will, as in a post-retirement verse at home (#127 "Staff in Hand") in which he enjoys his freedom to indulge in hiking and appreciating nature's beautiful scenery, then returns home and goes straight to bed,

but the pros and cons of kings and tyrants
still invade my dreams
and let me know that ways long set
are not forgotten yet.

This is a great example of the dream functioning to resist the poet's post-retirement effort to forget his years of striving to achieve a just society, his many setbacks and failures as a reformer, but now finally able to focus on his own quest for enlightenment through Zen Buddhist practice. Ironically, the dream here becomes a medium for realism to intrude into his post-retirement fantasy of enjoying an enlightened Zen lifestyle.

有时候，梦对他是一种刺激，因为与他的意志相反。《杖藜》（127）是他隐退后在家写的，诗中提到他非常喜欢可以自由自在地游山玩水，然后回家就上床休息：“尧桀是非时入梦，固知余习未全忘。”这首诗是个很好的例子，说明梦不让他忘记那么多年他要建造公平社会的努力、他改革的挫折和失败。而他终于可以集中精力通过禅宗佛教追求觉悟。然而，这里的梦成了现实的媒介，介入他隐退后梦想享受文明的禅式生活。

The role or motive of a dream, however, is not always so obvious as the above examples. Sometimes the dream may convey a more subtle sense of irony, a sweet and subtle sadness, as in these lines, composed at the end of a delightful nap (#21 "A Nap"):

A peeping bird calls
to my gracefully drifting dream
a sweet and subtle sadness fed
by mountains beyond the stream.

The peeping bird call launches the blurred and indeterminate threshold that divides the subjective dreamscape and objective landscape. Wang's comfort with the poetry of unclear distinctions is consistent with his Zen Buddhist beliefs that binary distinctions are illusory.

梦的作用和动机并不总如上述那般明显。有时候梦会传达一种隐约的讽刺感，一种“宛转愁”，就如《午枕》（21）一诗中说道：“窥人鸟唤悠扬梦，隔水山供宛转愁。”诗中的窥人鸟的叫声设下了主观的梦境与客观的现实景色的模糊不清的界限。王安石对诗中的模糊不清感受到的安逸与其“禅宗佛家相信黑白不分明”的信念是一致的。

Having noted the Zen Buddhist belief that binary distinctions are illusory, we still find in Wang's poetry that dreams are most often seen as groundless fantasies, the opposite of "reality." In one poem (#63 "When I Was Young") he states this unambiguously: "To me, spring's return is unreal as a dream." Elsewhere (#107), in describing a "ghost town," he observes: "A hundred years have brought it down like a shattered dream that was." In another poem (#117 A Conversation with Geng Tianzhi) he alludes to "the Handan Dream," also known as "the Yellow Millet Dream," in which a poor scholar spends a whole lifetime in a dream, then wakes up to discover that the yellow millet on the stove is not yet fully cooked.

In a poem (#118) entitled "Composed in a Dream," when Wang sees that menacing rain clouds are moving in from the north, he also notices a wine shop with huge cabinets filled with jugs of wine. When the downpour makes rainwaters rise "axle-high" on the road, he wryly observes: "Not selling the wine doesn't worry me, / I just worry that this dream will cease to be." This observation requires us to adopt two perspectives at once – as a participant within the dreamscape, and as an outside observer with a sense of humor.

禅宗中认为黑白分明的二元制是虚幻的。王安石诗中的梦常常还是莫须有的幻觉，正是“现实”的相反。在《少年见青春》（63）一诗中，他明确地写道：“春归只如梦”。另外，在《孤城》（107）中，他观察到“百年颠倒如梦寐”。他更在另一首诗《与耿天骘会话》（117）中提到邯郸梦，也叫黄粱梦，说到卢生如何在梦中过了一生，醒来后，连煮上的黄粱还没熟呢：“邯郸四十余年梦，相对黄粱欲熟时。”

在《梦中作》（118）中，王安石看见北边黑云密布，天将雨，又注意到附近一家酒铺，其大柜中装满了酒罐。当路上雨水淹到有“车轴”高时，他讽刺地说：“独龙注雨如车轴，不畏不售畏不续。”这一说法要我们同时采取两种观点：又是梦境中的参与者，又是富有幽默感的旁观者。

Of course, we also find in Wang's poems an example of the worldwide folk belief that dreams can foretell of future events. In his poem (#19) "In Memory of Wang Fengyuan," Wang Anshi notes that Wang Fengyuan passed away when his wife was expecting a child, and sympathetically observes: "A good man's family should endure, so I know she must 'dream of bears.'" In ancient Chinese folklore, dreaming of bears was believed to predict the birth of a male heir. Wang mentions this because it gives some assurance that Wang Fengyuan's lineage can continue, and his posterity will be able to make offerings to his spirit.

We know that Buddhists strive to develop and maintain a non-dualistic mindset, because dualistic, "either-or" binary mindsets eventually lead to false dichotomies. Wang was acutely aware of this, as we see in one of his 20 poems in the style of Han Shan and Shi De (#128), where he chides himself for his judgmental feelings that arise at the very sight of Zhang San, returns home and repents, then feels the same discriminating urge the next time he sees Zhang San, leading him to conclude that:

If this bad habit could be put down
there'd be very few Buddhists around.

This implies that if we could control the urge to discriminate, there would be little use for Buddhist practices.

当然，在王安石的诗中，我们也看到世人广泛存在的信念：梦会预报未来。在《思王逢原》（19）一诗中，他提到王逢原去世时，王的妻子正怀着孕。所以，他非常同情地写道："贤者宜有后，固当梦熊罴。"中国古代民间相信梦见"熊罴"意味着会生男孩。因为生男孩，王逢原就有继承人，后代就有人为他的灵魂烧香。

我们都知道佛家都要尽量做到非二元制的想法，因为二元制"黑白分明"的想法和观念最终会达到虚假的黑白分明的二分法。王安石很了解这一点。在他的《拟寒山拾得二十首（其十）》（128）中，他怪自己一看到张三就想批评他，而一回家就又很懊悔。然而，下次看到张三又想歧视他。终于他下结论道："若除此恶习，佛法无多子。"意思是说，如果我们都能控制歧视别人的心，那就没什么人需要练佛家的功了。

We also observe that the threshold between fantasy and reality in Wang's poetry may be presented in the form of the gradual ending of a dream, as in "Nap at Noon" (#72):

Vague remnants of a noonday dream
and then, from somewhere, an oriole.

and again in "Garden of Enlightenment" (#92):

a dream by the window fades
to bird calls at noon.

As a serious lay Buddhist and lay Taoist, Wang understood that what most people call "reality" is in fact a human concept and construct that can only be understood in binary opposition to another human concept called "fantasy." An enlightened adept will actually revel in the mysterious realm of neither-nor rather than the mundane realm of either-or, which can be found in the midst of gradual awakening from a dream. It can also be intentionally created through meditation on that mysterious state, as we see in the concluding lines of Wang's poem "Climbing Baogong Pagoda" (#126):

Here, notions like guest and host
are hardly ever heard,
the priest forgets about the "I"
and I forget the word.

我们也注意到王安石诗中，幻觉与现实的界限可能以梦渐醒的形式呈现。如在这首《午睡》（72）中所述：“悠然残午梦，何许一黄鹂。”还有《悟真院》（92）中的“午窗残梦鸟相呼”。王安石是认真的世俗佛家，也是认真的世俗道家。他很了解一般人所谓的“现实”其实只是人类打造出来的观念；只有与另一种人类的观念即“幻觉”对照时才能了解它。达到觉悟的内行人其实会陶醉于不是黑白分明的境界里，而不会欣赏世俗的黑白分明的境界。这种诗人陶醉的境界存在于渐醒的梦中，也可以存在于那神秘的静修时。王安石的诗《登宝公塔》（126）就有“当此不知谁客主，道人忘我我忘言”。

We hope our readers will enjoy, as we have, both the poems and the various forms and levels of Wang Anshi's ideals and dreams.

Finally, we would like to thank our editor, Ms. Li Shasha, and Ms. Liu Lingling who completed the inspired illustrations for all of the poems. Last but not least, we are grateful to the New World Press for bringing this copy to the world.

Jan W. Walls and Yvonne L. Walls
January 31, 2019
Vancouver, Canada

在此希望读者能与我们共享王安石的诗词，以及他的各种形式和各层次的理想和梦境。

最后，我们感谢编辑李莎莎和画家柳玲玲对此书的贡献，更感谢新世界出版社使这本书顺利问世。

王健　李盈

2019 年 1 月 31 日

加拿大 温哥华

图书在版编目（CIP）数据

空鸟迹：王安石诗词中英本 / (加) 王健 (Jan W. Walls)，(加) 李盈 (Yvonne L. Walls) 编译；柳玲玲绘图. -- 北京：新世界出版社，2019.6
ISBN 978-7-5104-6810-0

Ⅰ. ①空⋯ Ⅱ. ①王⋯ ②李⋯ ③柳⋯ Ⅲ. ①古典诗歌—诗集—中国—北宋—汉、英 Ⅳ. ① I222.744.1

中国版本图书馆 CIP 数据核字 (2019) 第 124717 号

BIRD TRACKS IN THE AIR
Selected Poems of Wang Anshi
空鸟迹
王安石诗词中英本

编　　译：〔加〕王健（Jan W. Walls）〔加〕李盈（Yvonne L. Walls）
绘　　图：柳玲玲
责任编辑：李莎莎
装帧设计：贺玉婷　王　珏
责任印制：王宝根　苏爱玲
出版发行：新世界出版社
社　　址：北京西城区百万庄大街 24 号（100037）
发 行 部：(010)6899 5968　(010)6899 8705（传真）
总 编 室：(010)6899 5424　(010)6832 6679（传真）
网　　址：http://www.nwp.cn
　　　　　http: //www.nwp.com.cn
版 权 部：+8610 6899 6306
版权电邮：nwpcd@sina.com
印　　刷：北京东方宝隆印刷有限公司
经　　销：新华书店
开　　本：880mm×1230mm　1/32
字　　数：243 千字　印张：11.375
版　　次：2019 年 6 月第 1 版　2019 年 6 月第 1 次印刷
书　　号：ISBN 978-7-5104-6810-0
定　　价：68.00 元